Buzz

A Steamy Small-Town Romance

Shelley Munro

For Paul.

Introduction

THE HEART KNOWS BEST...

Jen Alexander is intent on fulfilling a promise to her mother. She's heading back to school to finish her education, but a remote-controlled vibrator shoves her on a detour.

For Wayne Garrett the night of Jen's party is a revelation. His strict rule of no sex with employees has blinded him to Jen's charms, but now that she no longer works for him he plans on seduction big time—a private party for three.

Divorced and depressed, Sebastian Lang refuses the idea of a threesome, worried his uncomfortable feelings for his best friend Wayne will pop into the open and spoil their friendship.

Wayne wants Jen. Sebastian wants Wayne. Jen doesn't want any man since her boyfriend ditched her by text minutes before her leaving party.

What is the best way to solve this dilemma? Laughter, fun and hot seduction helps the trio to decide exactly what they want and how to maneuver past jealousy and preconceptions to achieve the ideal solution in this friends to lovers romance.

Contains helpful friends, a bitchy ex-wife, school cliques and assignments, small town noisiness and the usual relationship ups and downs times three.

Chapter One

"SEBASTIAN."

A sharp elbow to Sebastian Lang's ribs jerked him off balance and he almost head-butted his date. He grasped her upper arms before she toppled on her arse in a chain reaction. "Sorry, sweetheart." He made sure she was okay before scowling at his friend Wayne, who hovered beside them. "What did you do that for?"

Wayne pantomimed something, frustration knitting his brow when Sebastian stared at him blankly. He tried again, his face screwing up until his expression resembled a tribal mask carved by one of his Māori ancestors. Obviously whatever Wayne wanted to say wasn't fit for a woman's ears.

"It's okay," the attractive blonde cooed, a heavy coating of mascara aiding her slow, sexy blink. "I'll give you some privacy 'cause I have to visit the little girls' room anyway."

Sebastian fought to restrain his grimace. *The little girls' room. Really?* Why didn't she call it a toilet and leave it at that? Everyone had to take a piss sometime. She waggled her fingers in a coy wave and sashayed away—or as much as she could sway wearing her tight little skirt and skyscraper heels.

"Sebastian!"

"What?" Sebastian glared at his longtime friend and business partner Wayne Garrett.

Wayne tore his gaze off the dance floor to study him properly. "What's crawled up your arse tonight?"

Nothing Wayne could fix. "What do you want?"

Wayne leaned closer, his tanned face alight with mischief. "Do you still have your remote control for the Fancy Free vibrator?"

"Not on me. It's in the office."

"Too bad. I persuaded Jocelyn to wear the vibrator tonight and noticed something interesting when I used the remote. Go and ask Jen for a dance."

Sebastian's brows rose. "Our Jen?"

Wayne grinned with his entire face. "I forgot that you haven't seen her yet. See the woman with the long, straight brown hair? The one wearing the short black skirt and pink top?"

Whoa! Nice arse. "That's Jen Alexander?"

"She cleans up good, huh? You should have seen her in shorts this morning. Made me feel way better about stopping by her house to pick up paperwork. I had no idea she was hiding that luscious body beneath her navy-blue suit."

"Stop." Sebastian held up his hand to enforce the harsh note in his voice. "That's Jen you're lusting over. She works for us and that makes her out of..." He trailed off, realizing what his friend was getting at. This was Jen's leaving party. After years of nursing her mother then working long hours to save money, she was going back to school full-time.

"Go and ask her to dance."

"Where's Giles? And where is Jocelyn?"

Wayne's face hardened, ice freezing his former humor. "Libby told me the bastard sent her a breakup text five minutes before she left for the party."

"A text? Prick better not come near me when we're working with Liam and Fletch's crew next week," Sebastian said with a growl. "And Jocelyn?"

"Jocelyn is in the kitchen talking to her cousin. Go before your date comes back from the *little girls' room*."

"You heard."

"Yep. You don't want her in your bed, Seb."

No, he didn't. He wanted Wayne. Sebastian shoved the thought aside, locking it firmly away and headed for Jen.

Thoughts like that had no business popping into his mind. Sighing, he weaved through the crowds of employees and friends on the dance floor. Laughter filled the Sloan town hall and the scent of hot sausage rolls floated on the air with the Women's Division matriarchs in the thick of the kitchen action.

"Jen?" Sebastian tapped her on the shoulder. "Would you like to dance?"

Jen turned and Sebastian got his first look at the miraculous transformation of their junior office assistant. Her curly hair no longer hung in uncontrolled chaos around her face. She must have visited a hairdresser because now it was dead straight and the shiny brown mass tumbled down her back. Her clothes were different too, showcasing a curvy body. Even her features looked different with an expert application of makeup.

"You look gorgeous, Jen." Not even her slightly reddened blue eyes detracted from her natural beauty. "Those high school boys aren't going to know what hit them."

"See! I told you." Gaby Montgomery, one of Jen's friends, sent her a thumbs-up.

Jen grinned, making her look more like the familiar Jennifer of the office. "I'm not going to school to check out the boys. I'm going to study. Besides, they're all at least seven years younger than me. When I date, I want a man—" She broke off suddenly, her good humor faltering, and Sebastian wanted to beat Giles to a pulp for hurting her.

He grabbed her hand. "Come and dance with me."

Jen found herself tugged into the midst of friends strutting their stuff on the floor. Sebastian put his arms around her, holding her lightly as they moved to the melody.

"We're going to miss you around the office."

"I'll still help Libby during my holidays." Somehow she didn't think Sebastian and Wayne would miss her in quite the same way she'd miss them. Her bosses were sexy men and in high demand with the single women living in and around the country town of Sloan. Local rumor said they'd used their building skills to install revolving doors on their bedrooms.

Not that she'd know. They treated her like a younger sister—which was as it should be, she reminded herself. Mind back on the plan.

Finish school. Accounting degree.

She didn't have time for a man in her life.

"That's good to hear." Sebastian smiled at her, ice blue eyes crinkling at the corners. "You know if you need anything all you have to do is ask."

"Thanks. I—" She broke off with a surprised gasp.

"What is it? What's wrong?"

"N-nothing," she said in a strangled voice. The new Fancy Free vibrator, the remote-controlled one she'd promised to test for her inventor friend Gaby, buzzed to life again. The very one she'd inserted minutes before Giles had so kindly sent her a text dumping her arse, vibrated on the perfect spot. She bit her bottom lip, concentrating on holding back her gasps of enjoyment. That felt *sooo* good.

The vibrations ceased as suddenly as they'd started. Thank god! That had been the second time tonight. She sucked in a hasty breath and glanced around for Giles. No, she was pretty sure he wasn't here. But she would be demanding back the remote control the second she saw the louse.

If he thought he could wriggle back into her good graces, he was sadly mistaken. No one treated her like a doormat and got away with it. And as soon as this dance ended, she'd make a hasty trip to the restrooms. If Gaby hadn't hustled her out of the house so quickly she'd have removed the vibrator before she'd left home. Since arriving at the hall, she hadn't managed a quiet moment to herself.

"What made you decide to change your hair?" Sebastian asked.

Jen frowned. Had he noticed her weird behavior?

"Jen?"

Oh dear. He would if she didn't act normally. "Libby gave me a voucher for the new beauty spa. Gaby dragged me off this afternoon and paid for a visit to the hairdresser."

"Giles is a fool."

"You heard?" Her gaze flew to his before flitting away in embarrassment. She didn't want his sympathy.

"Jen, look at me." His imperious tone brooked no refusal and his callused fingertips tipping her face upward sealed the deal. "You're better off without the idiot."

The insistent buzz in her pussy started again. She groaned, saw his eyes widen and suspicions start to coalesce.

"What else did Gaby give you?"

"Nothing." The stimulation intensified. Chills chased across her flesh and for one horrid moment she thought her knees would buckle. Another quick punch of heat forced a moan from her.

"Giles better not have control of that remote," Sebastian said in a snarl.

A full-body flush replaced her former chill and she tried to look away. He wouldn't let her.

"Jen?"

"Giles told me he wasn't coming to the party. I don't

11

know who has the remote," she almost wailed. And if she found out, she'd kill them. "I need to go to the restroom."

"We're both grown-ups," he whispered, gathering her closer when she tried to yank from his touch. His scent washed over her—something exotic and sexy. Enticement for a woman to snuggle close. His body heat seared her while the vibrations and the nifty attachment stimulated her clit. She whimpered, her fingers digging into his shoulders. Pleasure coursed through her body, followed swiftly by excruciating mortification. She bit down on her inner cheek, desperate to contain her sounds of enjoyment. God, she'd never live this down.

"Let's go." Sebastian pulled away abruptly and hauled her off the dance floor.

Every step abraded her clit until, thankfully, the vibrations stopped. She sagged against Sebastian, taking deep, shuddering breaths.

He took most of her weight and dragged her out the side door of the hall into the cool evening air. Jen was glad of the gloom because her face glowed with humiliation—she just knew it. This was her boss and she was practically climaxing in his arms. Even worse, he *knew*.

"You should go back inside and spend time with your girlfriend." *Yes, please!* She'd never manage to meet his gaze again. The second he left her alone, she'd whip out the vibrator. She'd never have agreed to wear the toy if she'd known *any* remote could turn it on. Next time Gaby persuaded her to try out one of her inventions she'd ask more questions. She'd demand full disclosure of the pertinent facts.

"I can't leave you like this."

"Yes, you can," she said firmly, cautiously shifting her weight. The vibrations had halted, and she relaxed a fraction. The remote must be out of range. Then, a familiar low pressure gathered between her legs. An intense burst of heat flashed through her, and another moan spilled from her lips. Her thighs clamped together, but if anything the move made things worse. She gasped, not willing to fall apart in front of her sexy boss.

"What are you doing out here?"

Great. Just great. Wayne, her other boss, was here too. Her embarrassment was complete. "Gaby talked me into trying out one of her vibrator designs."

"Why are you telling us?" Wayne asked.

Something in his smooth voice aroused her suspicions. "You!" She advanced on Wayne and poked her finger into the middle of his chest. "You have the remote. You're doing this to me."

Almost before she finished speaking, the vibrations started again, relentless in their intensity. Wayne took one look at her pained grimace and drew her into his arms, despite her objections.

Sebastian crowded her from behind, nuzzling her neck with his lips. He nipped her earlobe, the sharp pain tossing her into a maelstrom of pleasure. Her clit pulsed and fire swarmed over her body, the convulsion into orgasm almost more than she could bear. She shuddered between the two hard male bodies. The pulses continued for a long time, intense and explosive, before trailing off.

Slowly, after luxuriating in the aftershocks, she came back to Earth. The vibrator stopped tormenting her. She'd say one thing for Gaby's newest invention—the toy packed a hell of a punch.

"Are you okay?" Wayne whispered.

"Why?" She glanced left and right. Where was the nearest rock? She'd like to crawl under it.

"You don't work for us anymore," Wayne said.

"What?" She didn't have to pretend indignation. "Does that make me fair game?"

"Of course not," Sebastian said smoothly.

"What do you want from me?" To say she was confused would have been an understatement. She felt as if someone had dumped her in Wonderland with Alice, where everything was topsy-turvy.

"I'd like to take you home," Wayne said without

hesitation.

"Why?" Jen cringed at her bluntness but it didn't seem to bother either of her bosses. *Ex-bosses,* she reminded herself.

"Wouldn't you like some hot, strings-free sex?" Wayne asked. "Imagine two men touching you, their hands wandering over your body. One lover sucking your breasts while the other licks your clit. One man crammed in your pussy while the other fucks your mouth or your arse. Think how good it would feel with two of us concentrating on your pleasure."

"Way to go, idiot." Sebastian clipped his friend across the side of his head. "Do you want to scare her off?"

The heat in her cheeks intensified and she forced herself to shrug, to pretend she didn't have the faintest idea about threesomes, while moisture coated her folds and renewed arousal simmered through her again. "What are you blathering about?"

Sebastian turned her to face him. "Come inside. We'll have a few drinks and dance a little."

"Good idea." Relief hit Jen. Once they were inside again their girlfriends would claim them. She brightened at the thought. Let their dates take them in hand and try to control them. She was heading straight to the restroom. Next up, she intended to do an online search for hit men and sic one on her best friend. "Let's go."

"Wait." Sebastian grasped her arm and spun her back to face him. His head dipped, and before she could protest, he had her in a lip-lock. Lips. Tongues. The whole nine yards.

"My turn."

She had a few seconds to take a quick breath before Wayne took over. His kiss was softer, not as intense, but it shoved her directly into confusion.

"What was that?" she asked in a near shriek, the second her lips were free. "Why?"

"Because we like you and we don't want you to go home and mope about that bastard Giles." Sebastian's gaze seemed to bore into her, searching out her insecurities.

A fickle breeze whistled down the alley, tugging playfully at his brown hair. She found herself reaching to smooth the unruly locks down and snatched her hand away, appalled by her loss of common sense.

"So you're giving me something else to stress about instead?" Her bosses had both kissed her, and not in a brotherly way. *Nowhere near brotherly.* She closed her eyes, counted to three. When she opened them again both men were still staring expectantly at her.

Wayne gripped her shoulders, slanting her to face him. "Wouldn't you like to thumb your nose at Giles? We could help you do that."

"Revenge isn't a good reason to lose my commonsense," Jen countered. "Besides, thanks to Gaby, I have several battery operated boyfriends to test. I don't need a man." Her gaze went from Wayne to Sebastian and back again. "Men," she amended since they seemed to come in a twin package.

"What about pleasure?" Sebastian asked.

"Hello? Battery operated boyfriends? Look, I don't know what the pair of you have been drinking, but I'm going back inside." Without a backward glance, she stomped into the hall, where the world was a much saner place.

Chapter Two

Wayne turned to Sebastian. "Are we going to let her get away with that?"

"We've both got dates tonight. We can hardly ditch them. That would put us on the same level as Giles."

"True." Wayne sighed before a brainwave struck. "Let's give her time to stew tonight and ambush her tomorrow."

"I like Jen, but why are you so interested in her all of a sudden?"

"It struck me this morning when I saw her. An epiphany. The perfect woman has been sitting under my nose. She's sexy yet sensible. She has a brain and doesn't agree with everything I say." The more he thought about romancing Jen, the better he liked the idea. "I like her a lot. She'd make a good wife and mother. What do you think? A little black-haired, brown-eyed mini-me." He paused. "Maybe they'll have Jen's blue eyes. It's possible."

"Don't you think you should run your ideas about marriage and children past Jen first? She's focused on getting her qualifications."

"I know. That's the downside from our point of view, but don't you think we could be good together?"

"Sure."

Sebastian's noncommittal reply bugged Wayne for the rest of the night and into the next morning. His friend was struggling with something. Wayne had no idea what the hell it was because, as usual, Sebastian was keeping his troubles close. He'd changed since his marriage but, thank god, Sebastian had come to his senses and called it quits on his union with Victoria, the barracuda. Maybe he was still healing or thought he was a failure. Some shit thing like that.

Movement behind him had Wayne reaching for the coffee pot. He sloshed coffee into a mug and shunted it across the table to Sebastian.

Wayne took in Sebastian's reddened eyes and the dark shadows underneath. Taken in conjunction with a day's stubble, it made him look like a thug. "You okay?"

Sebastian grunted, his hand curling around the coffee mug.

"Didn't you sleep?"

"No."

"Want to go out for brunch?"

Sebastian glanced up from his coffee, cast him a look. "You buyin'?"

"Yep." Wayne drained the last of his coffee and stood. "Let's go."

"Are you still going ahead with your plan to woo Jen?"

Wayne tested the idea of abandoning his scheme. He scowled, not liking it at all. "Yes. It's a good move."

Sebastian set his mug down and rose. "You'll want me to shift out then. Find my own place."

"Hell no." Wayne didn't even have to think about it. "You're like my brother, man. Closer than a brother. I figured we'd woo Jen together. Blue-eyed kids would work too." To Wayne's astonishment, Sebastian clenched his fists. He looked as if he wanted to flatten him. "What? What have I said wrong?"

"A threesome isn't normal." Sebastian's pale eyes flashed with temper. "Not if you want marriage and kids. Besides, don't you think Jen should have a say in the matter? Way I heard it, she's off men at present. She refused to speak to either of us after we went back inside the hall last night."

"Jen never holds a grudge."

"There's always a first time. Are we doing brunch or not?" Sebastian grabbed the keys to his truck and stomped out the door.

Wayne stared after his friend before slowly following. He'd get to the bottom of whatever was chafing Sebastian's butt eventually.

"I'M NOT TALKING TO you," Jen said the second Gaby joined her at the corner table of the Sloan cafe.

"What did I do?" Gaby batted her dark eyelashes, trying to pull off innocent. She didn't come close.

"You could have warned me about the remotes for your vibrators." She glanced around the café and leaned closer to whisper, "Other people's remotes worked on my vibrator."

Gaby clapped a hand over her mouth, but not quickly enough to hide her smirk. Caught in the act, she gave up trying to hold back her amusement. Her throaty chuckle rang out, attracting way too much attention for Jen's peace of mind. When Gaby managed to pull herself together, she asked, "Um, do you know who had the remote?"

"Wayne and Sebastian." This time a grim tone shaded her voice. Her bosses. Of all people! Sex and her bosses together in the same sentence. That was dangerous territory. Nope, not going there.

"Both of them?"

Agh! "Yes." And she still couldn't believe the way she'd trembled and shivered in their arms. "I've never been so embarrassed in all my life, and it's your fault. I heard your lecture about making sure I was on the Pill just in case the condoms broke, but I'm positive you never warned me about interchangeable remotes!"

The doorbell tinkled, indicating that more customers had arrived.

Gaby glanced up briefly before turning her attention back to Jen. With her black spiral curls and dancing eyes she looked the picture of an irrepressible imp. "Don't you like them?"

"Of course I like them but that's not the point."

"What is the point, sweetheart?" The masculine drawl jerked Jen upright. Her spine struck the back of her wood and chrome chair.

"They're standing right behind me. Aren't they?" Jen glared an accusation at Gaby. "You could have warned me." Her head jerked around so rapidly it was a wonder she didn't suffer whiplash. "You two always pop out of the woodwork at the perfect time to cause me maximum embarrassment."

"Pull up a seat," Gaby said. "We're about to order."

"I'm sure they have better things to do," Jen said, glowering at the two men before focusing on her traitorous friend.

"Not really." Wayne's brown eyes twinkled with mischief. The perfect foil for his shiny black hair. No doubt about it. The scalawag Māori god Maui must hover in his DNA. *Excellent. Pair him with Gaby, and Jen had a matching set of imps.*

More serious with ice blue eyes and brutally short brown hair, Sebastian didn't say anything, merely pulled out a chair and planted his muscular butt.

Gaby clapped her hands together. "That's settled then."

"You mean you want to witness them tormenting me. Newsflash, boys. No vibrator today." Her voice had risen and heat galloped into her cheeks when she noticed the elderly women at the next table whispering to each other. She lowered her voice. "End of discussion."

"No need to worry. We have plenty of sex toys at home," Wayne informed her. "You can take your pick."

Jen's breath caught, and it was nothing to do with the mention of sex toys. It was the temptation to nod and agree to the crazy proposition. Food. That might fix her lightheadedness. "Breakfast is not the right time to discuss sex toys."

"It's closer to lunch," Wayne said, after a swift glance at his watch.

"I discuss sex toys all day, every day," Gaby piped up.

"Quiet in the cheap seats." Jen lowered her gaze and studied her menu. She knew it by heart, but she was frightened to witness their expressions. "What is everyone doing this afternoon? I'm going to work in the garden and mow the lawn before the place becomes even more of a jungle. I won't have as much time once the school term starts the week after next." Hmm, a fry-up or something healthy?

"Fletch and Liam are working this morning," Gaby said, mentioning her two men. "We might go for a swim at the river later if the sun keeps shining. I was thinking a picnic dinner since the days are so long now. You should come too. All of you."

"Tempting, but the gardening is a big job. I doubt I'll finish in time."

"I'll mow your lawns," Sebastian said. "Wayne is visiting his family."

"True. I'd help, but it's my mother's birthday," Wayne said.

Jen jerked her attention from the coffee-splattered menu. "You don't have to help me. I'm sure you have better things to do."

"Don't argue," Sebastian said, his tone final.

Jen's lips pressed together, keeping her words of protest trapped behind her teeth. For reasons unknown the powers that be had decided to give her a hard time this week. "Fine," she gritted out, showing none of the gratitude such an offer would normally attract. "If you want to get all hot and sweaty it's no skin off my nose."

"Sounds dirty," Gaby said.

"Shut up," Jen snapped. "It's not too late for me to order a hit man and set him on you."

"You're a bloodthirsty wench," Wayne said. "We'll have to watch you."

"If you'd stop picking on me, you wouldn't need to worry about hit men," Jen snapped.

"Ah, can I take your order now?" The young waitress edged away from Jen, her eyes wide and wary.

Heck, where had she come from? Calm breaths. *In. Out. In. Out.* All she needed to do was get through one lousy breakfast. How difficult could it be?

What followed next was an entire hour of teasing and leg-pulling, a lot of it at her expense. Gaby and Wayne were in top form while Sebastian appeared tired and plain grumpy, not contributing more than the odd grunt.

They left the cafe together, splitting up when they reached the small car park at the rear of the building. Jen's house wasn't far and she'd walked. She waved goodbye and set off, striding past the dress shop and the jeweler's. Mrs. George, the florist, was busy setting out her buckets of pastel-colored stocks, and Jen sniffed appreciatively as she waved hello.

A vehicle sounded behind her. Instead of speeding past, it slowed.

"Jen, I'm gonna drop off Wayne. I'll be at your place in half an hour," Sebastian called.

"You don't have to mow my lawn."

"Don't argue," Wayne said.

"Jen," Sebastian said.

Her name held a warning and she gave an irritable shrug. "Whatever." Jen stormed away from his truck, feeling as if her life were careering out of control. She continued her stomping all the way home. Stupid man.

In her bedroom, she changed into a pair of denim shorts and a tank top. She slapped a cap on her head and collected a trowel and a pair of gardening gloves from the garden shed at the rear of her house. Thankfully she only had one garden left to weed, the big one out the front. When her mother was still alive this garden had always been ablaze with color every summer, and the fragrant scent of sweet peas had filled the air.

Sebastian pulled up in the driveway ten minutes later. He climbed out, still wearing a frown and looking like hell. "Where's the mower?"

"In the garden shed at the rear of the house. The petrol

can is there too."

He gave her a clipped nod and stalked off. The man could be moody, yet he was always fair with his employees. Even so, he seemed worse than normal. Shaking away her curiosity, she returned to the garden bed and weeding.

In the distance, the motor mower roared to life, and Jen started to yank both weeds and the remnants of old plants from the soil. Part of her wanted to replant the garden with sweet peas to hold the memory of her mother close. Yet common sense told her to fill the garden with no-fuss succulents. She wouldn't need to water them much, and if she put down weed mat and pebbles, she'd save herself time when it came to weeding.

Changes.

Jen sighed and rotated her neck and shoulders to ease the tension that came from remaining in one spot for too long. She resumed pulling weeds. Moving on with her life was good. It was what her mother had wanted for her.

Half an hour later the roar of the mower came closer as Sebastian started to mow the strip of lawn along the side of the house. From where she was weeding, she couldn't help but notice that he'd removed his shirt and tucked it into the back pocket of his jeans. The black T-shirt trailed after him like a tail, but it was his sweaty torso, glinting in the sunshine, that grabbed her attention. *Wow. Just wow.*

Muscles rippled as he pushed the mower in a methodical pattern around the lawn.

A car slowed and turned into her driveway. She jerked her attention off Sebastian to face her visitor. Giles? What the heck did he want? Surely he'd said everything the evening before in his terse text?

Jen removed her gardening gloves and stood, brushing the seat of her shorts with her hands as she went to meet Giles. Since he was here he could return the remote she'd given him for the vibrator.

"Giles, what are you doing here?" she shouted, in an attempt to be heard above the mower.

The mower stopped, leaving an uneasy silence and the ring of her voice.

Giles smiled broadly. "I wanted to ask you out for dinner."

"You broke up with me last night. By text." Her eyes narrowed on him. "You didn't have the guts to do it in person."

"Look, babe. I'm sorry. I made a mistake. Let me take you out to dinner and make it up to you."

Jen's fists clenched at her sides. "Where were you thinking of eating?"

"We'll go to the inn. It's expensive but you're worth it."

"Where did you go last night?" Her fingernails dug into

her palms.

"I had a migraine," Giles said. "Seb, mate. What are you doing here? I didn't realize you were having money problems and had started mowing lawns." His ringing laughter was plain malicious.

"Lying bastard," Sebastian snapped from behind her. "I saw you with Rachel, down by the river last night when I drove past. You didn't have a headache." He took a couple of rapid steps toward Giles, but Jen grabbed Sebastian's arm and dug in her heels until he stopped his advance.

Giles retreated rapidly, his shoulders becoming tense with wariness.

"Don't hit him," she said to Sebastian. She turned her attention back to Giles. "Sebastian is helping me with the garden work."

"Why not? He treated you like crap."

"Do *not* hit him. Giles, do you have the remote control for my vibrator?"

"Yeah, it's in the car." Giles regained his confidence and smirked, his brows going up and down in a suggestive manner. "Should I push the power button?" His gaze wandered from her face, down her form-fitting T-shirt to linger at her crotch.

"Could I have it please?" She smiled pleasantly.

"Right now?"

"Yes please."

Giles shrugged and opened his door to paw through the junk covering the passenger seat. "Ah, here it is." He handed it over, letting his hand linger on hers during the transfer.

"Thank you." Jen repressed a shudder at his touch.

"So how about dinner tonight? And maybe afterward we could experiment with the toys Gaby is always giving you." He smiled and placed his hands on her shoulders.

She shook them off. "I don't think so, Giles. You're a no-good, two-timing rat, and I wouldn't date you again if you were the last man in New Zealand."

Shock flickered across Giles' face, swiftly followed by anger. "I was only using you for sex," he snarled.

"Is that right?"

A dangerous growl sounded behind her.

"And you're not even good at that," Giles added.

Jen's fist lashed out before the thought even registered. She struck his nose with a loud, satisfying crunch.

"Ow!" Blood poured down Giles' face and splattered over his cotton shirt. He cradled his nose and moaned pitifully.

"You should go," Jen said.

"I'll press charges. I have a witness."

"I didn't see a thing," Sebastian said. "I was tying my

bootlace."

Giles cursed and stumbled around to the driver's door of his vehicle, still holding his nose. A few minutes later he drove off, steering with one hand and holding a wad of tissues to stem his bleeding nose.

"How come you told me not to hit him?"

"Because if anyone was going to hit him I wanted it to be me." Jen didn't move until Giles' car disappeared around the corner. Then she folded up, a whimper of pain escaping her compressed lips. "I think I've broken my hand."

Chapter Three

"You can't do any more weeding. You might as well have an early dinner with me," Sebastian said, glancing over at her as he drove from the doctor's office and turned onto the main street of Sloan. He'd always liked her feistiness. Hell, he couldn't believe she'd hit Giles. His mouth twitched at the memory but he wasn't dumb enough to let her see his amusement.

"You don't have to nursemaid me. You heard the doctor say that nothing's broken."

"He also told you to rest your hand."

"But I've got so many things to do before I start school. I didn't expect to waste my afternoon waiting to see the doctor."

"Tomorrow," Sebastian said firmly. "We'll pick up your prescription for pain relief, and I'll cook you dinner at Wayne's place."

"Just because you held me during an orgasm it doesn't give you the right to tell me what to do. You're not the boss of me. I quit, remember?"

Sebastian pulled up outside the pharmacy. "You didn't quit. You handed in your notice. Where's your prescription? It will be quicker if I run in and collect it."

"You never used to be such a tyrant."

"Because you used to behave with a modicum of sense," Sebastian retorted. "Prescription. Now."

"Bully." She slapped it onto his palm.

When he returned with the pills she was hunched up, her eyes closed. Her hair was straight again today, but a few errant brown curls were attempting to spring forth at her temples. Her cheeks were pale, a marked change from earlier. He started up his vehicle and headed for home. Wayne's house. He didn't have a home now.

When they arrived Jen was asleep. Wayne hadn't returned from his visit yet because his vehicle wasn't in the driveway, but it didn't matter. His best friend wanted Jen. He wouldn't mind if Sebastian persuaded her to stay the night.

Of course he might be a little pissed if Jen spent the night in Sebastian's bed, but he'd be damned if he intended to spend the night sleeping on the couch. It was about six inches too short for his six foot three inch frame for a start, and the leather was slippery and uncomfortable during the summer heat.

"Jen, we're here."

When she didn't answer, he climbed out and jogged around to the passenger side. After unfastening the seatbelt, he bent to lift her out.

"What are you doing?"

"Taking you inside. You've been overdoing things," he added, his tone skimming along the edges of accusation.

"I can walk. I'm not an invalid."

A snort escaped him. "I don't think I've ever met such a contrary woman. You weren't like this in the office. You're worse than my ex."

"I'm nothing like your ex."

All true. Jen didn't have a deceitful bone in her body. "But you are obstinate."

"There's nothing wrong with independence."

"There's nothing wrong with accepting help from a friend either."

A crinkle creased her forehead. "Are we friends?"

"Yes." And soon they'd be more if Wayne had his way. Wayne thought she'd be right for both of them. The truth was that although he'd protested, he'd agree with almost anything Wayne suggested if it meant he could spend time with his best friend. Sad but true. "Yes, we're friends."

"I'm not sure men and women can be friends without sex messing everything up."

"Are you saying we're gonna have sex?"

"I— No! You're twisting my words. You need to feed me. I have low blood sugar," she muttered. "Cripes, normally I'm better at self-censoring."

"How much did you censor while working for us?" he asked, genuinely curious.

"Not telling."

"I'll worm it out of you later or set Wayne on you. He'll charm the truth from you."

"I'm immune," she said with a trace of smugness. "You can't pull that crap on me."

"We'll see." Sebastian helped her out of his truck, taking a moment to grab her pain pills before he guided her inside.

"Do you want to watch me make dinner or do you want to lie down?"

"For the last time, I'm not an invalid. I'll sit at the breakfast counter. What are you making for dinner?"

Sebastian opened the fridge to peer inside. "Penne pasta with salmon, mushrooms and asparagus in a cream sauce. Maybe a salad on the side or some garlic bread."

"You can make that?"

"Don't sound so surprised." Sebastian pulled several items out of the fridge and set them on the counter. "It doesn't take much to cook a meal."

"I could have gone home, you know. You didn't have to kidnap me."

"Maybe I was lonely and wanted some company."

"Humph!"

"I'm not like Wayne," Sebastian said. "After the divorce—never mind. Do you want a drink of something? Orange juice or water."

"Give me alcohol. I'll take a beer," Jen said.

Sebastian returned to the fridge and grabbed two bottles of beer. He opened them both and handed one to Jen. Bemused, he watched her drink. His ex wouldn't have been seen dead holding a beer, let alone drinking one. He took a swallow of his before setting it aside and starting to chop an onion. "What else is on your to-do list? Maybe I could help."

"You don't have to help me. I've been looking after myself for a long time now."

Sebastian paused with the knife action. "Did you ever think that I might be at a loose end and would like to fill my time helping a friend?"

"What about your women and the revolving door on your bedroom?"

Sebastian crushed a clove of garlic with the flat of his knife, disposed of the paperlike covering and started to chop it into small dice. If only she knew. "That's Wayne's bedroom, not mine."

"Don't tell fibs. I've seen you with lots of different women."

"That doesn't mean I sleep with them." Silent questions floated in the air, and he could feel her gaze drilling into his back as he turned away.

"Your ex-wife hurt you," she said finally.

"There were faults on both sides."

"What sort of faults?"

She was being nosy, but he knew nothing he said would emerge on the Sloan gossip web. "We shouldn't have married in the first place. You know my parents died when I was three years old?"

"Yeah, I know you and Wayne met in foster care when you were five."

"I thought I'd make a home with Victoria. A life. But it turned out we wanted different things."

"A home takes work. It's not just a house. It's the people and the love they have for each other that makes a home." Her voice held warmth and empathy. It twisted through him, taking root in an unused portion of his heart. Why hadn't he met someone like Jen when he'd needed it most?

"Wise words." He kept his attention on the mushrooms he was slicing. "I wish I'd realized that back then."

"What are you going to do now?"

Sebastian knew she wasn't talking about cooking the piece of salmon he'd unwrapped. He paused, trying not to flinch at the thought of the long road of nothingness that stretched before him.

"I don't know." The truth emerged before he could think up some bullshit answer. He couldn't stay with Wayne forever. For his sanity's sake, he'd leave. Wayne said he didn't mind Sebastian crashing at his place, but he had to move on, and soon, before he did something stupid to sever their long-time friendship. "We've got a lot of work lined up. We'll be busy until at least the end of the year."

"Hmm," Jen said. "Which way is the toilet?"

"Through that door, second on the right."

She nodded and he watched her walk from the kitchen, sensing he'd disappointed her with his answer. The truth was he didn't have a clue. Work filled his days and some of his weekends, and since his divorce, he'd played hard during his downtime, dating lots of women. Sleeping with a few of them. It had gotten old fast.

Sebastian put on a pot of water to boil for the pasta and started to fry the onion and mushrooms.

"Which room is yours?"

Sebastian looked up. "Someone's been snooping."

"Yeah." She smirked as she slid onto the stool again. "I

had to check out the famous revolving doors."

"Guess."

"Well, Wayne is the messy one, but both rooms are tidy." She scanned his face, her gaze like a physical touch. His breath caught at the unfamiliar sensations coursing through him. Happiness. Confusion because the feeling was so foreign.

"Mrs. Partington does cleaning for Wayne once a week. She normally comes on Friday but this week she came yesterday, which is why Wayne's room is still relatively tidy."

Jen nodded. "I didn't know you liked to read."

"Good guess." A large bookcase filled one wall of his bedroom, and it was crammed full of books.

"How do you like the e-reader?"

His brows rose. "You did snoop."

"Answer my question. I was thinking of getting one."

"I tend to buy more ebooks these days. There's a big selection available and I don't need to worry about storage."

"What do you read?"

"Just about anything. Go and get my ereader and try it out."

"Thanks!" Jen beamed and jumped off the stool. She returned moments later and perched at the breakfast bar, muttering a little when she forgot and tried to use her right hand. "Oh my god. You're reading an erotic romance."

"It was free." And it was actually quite good.

"A threesome. Kinky."

"Do you think three people can have a relationship?" The question popped out before he curtailed the thought.

Her head jerked up, her eyes rounding as she stared at him. "It works in stories."

"Yes." *Wow, that was a real smooth introduction. Exactly why I should leave this stuff to Wayne.* Shock followed swiftly. What? Was he actually considering Wayne's crazy idea?

"Gaby, Liam and Fletch seem happy."

"You haven't answered my question."

Heat suffused her cheeks, and she couldn't meet his intense gaze any longer. She focused on the ereader's screen. "I'm too busy for romance."

"Coward."

She looked at him then, searching his expression, trying to work out what he wanted from her. Was he suggesting a threesome? Or was it a random question because of the story he was reading? "I think it takes three very special people to have that sort of relationship. There's a lot of trust involved, and I think it would be easy for jealousy to creep into the equation. Gaby says open communication is the key."

"Could you?" Damn, one strike already. According to his ex, he sucked at expressing his feelings.

"Is this about last night?" She waited impatiently while Sebastian added the penne to the boiling water. "About Wayne wanting me to come here with both of you?" She'd felt so safe when she'd stood between them, pleasure gripping her body. It had been nice to lean on someone else for a change. Her blush intensified but she forced herself to scrutinize him, to watch every flicker of expression.

"It's difficult enough trying to keep one person happy, let alone two."

"But you'd have two people to share your troubles."

He forced a grin. "Two people to kiss and caress."

Jen frowned at him, fiddled with the label of her beer bottle. "Would you really do it? Have sex with two people at once?"

Sebastian took the vegetables off the heat and added a salmon fillet to the pan. It sizzled as the skin met the hot surface. "Permanently?" He turned to her with a shrug. "It would depend on the circumstances and the people involved. I'd have to trust them."

"So you'd go into the situation after thinking it through. It wouldn't be impulsive for you."

"I like sex as much as the next guy. I've had sex since

my divorce but the connection is only fleeting. I want more." Pain flickered in him as he said the words and her heart twisted. Here was a guy who wanted marriage and probably fatherhood, yet his wife had screwed him. Most women would kill for a man who wanted to settle down and grow roots. It was a pity they were at different stages in their lives, because men like Sebastian were rare.

Jen picked up her beer and swallowed the last mouthful. "Would you choose two women or would you want a man and a woman?"

"I've had one threesome and that was with Wayne and a woman."

"Who?" Nosy interest slipped the question out before she buttoned her lips.

"The who isn't important."

He didn't intend to tell her. Tick on the approval rating. "Did you talk the encounter to death before you did anything?"

He flipped the salmon, his snort sounding over the renewed sizzle of the pan. "No we did not. We drank too much and things developed from there."

"Are you still friends with the woman?"

"We don't see her much these days. In the light of the day, she wasn't very comfortable with the three-way. She accused us of getting her drunk on purpose."

"Did you?"

"What's with all the questions?"

"I like to know what makes people tick. This isn't work, so I can be as interested as I want. So did you ply her with alcohol?"

"Do you think that's something either Wayne or I would do? Do you?" His voice rose toward the end of his sentence, and he waved his spatula in time with his abrupt words.

"There's no need to get defensive."

"Anyone I sleep with knows the score ahead of time." His level gaze drove the point home. "And I don't need to get them drunk. What sort of books do you like to read?"

Jen accepted the change of subject even though she wanted to ask more nosy questions. "I like mysteries and thrillers. Romance is okay, but I like to have a mystery angle combined with the romance. I doubt I'll have much time to read for pleasure once school starts."

"Are you nervous?"

"Not yet. I probably will be when I walk into the classroom for the first time."

Sebastian handed her another beer. "You'll be fine once you settle in, although I'm glad it's not me. I hated school."

"Why?"

"I lived in a foster home. That made me stand out."

Jen laughed, and it held a nervous tinge. "Don't tell me about different. I'm terrified enough about joining a class."

"Ah, but you're choosing to go to school. I only went to eat my lunch. Would you like to have a glass of wine with your dinner?"

Obviously another touchy subject, one she couldn't let pass. "You're not stupid, Sebastian. You and Wayne have built up a successful business. That takes brains and initiative."

He snorted. "You didn't see the comments on my school report. Have you seen any good movies lately?"

"No, I've been concentrating on getting everything shipshape at home. It's such a big house to look after on my own. I've been thinking about selling and buying something smaller."

"But?"

"Alexanders have lived there for four generations. Mum inherited it from her parents when they died, and it's full of memories of my mother and my childhood. I don't know. My head tells me selling is a good idea while my heart sings a different tune."

Sebastian flaked the salmon and added it to the drained pasta. Fascinated, Jen watched him put the dish together and garnish it with fresh basil. He made it look effortless, and watching him did something to her, made her see him differently. No, that wasn't quite the truth. The change had occurred last night when he'd held her so tenderly and kissed her neck while she'd fallen apart at the seams.

He was a good man even if he didn't see himself that way.

"If you need help to do anything around the house, let me know. Okay?"

She nodded, silently placating him even though she had no intention of asking for assistance.

"Verbal agreement," he said with a meaningful rise of eyebrows.

"Yes," she said crossly.

"Good." Sebastian set out placemats and cutlery at the breakfast bar. "I think we'll drink Wayne's bottle of wine with our dinner. Here, take these." He handed her a bowl of pasta and she winced a bit at the throb of pain in her hand.

A few minutes later, Sebastian took the seat opposite her.

Jen swallowed a mouthful of the pasta. "This is delicious."

"You sound surprised."

"I am. None of the men I've dated could cook."

"I used to hide out in the kitchens at the foster home. The cook said if I stayed there I had to work."

"Hide out?"

"I was small as a child. The other kids picked on me."

"I'm sorry."

"Why?" Sebastian sounded surprised. "There's always a pecking order amongst kids. Besides, Wayne stuck up for me."

Conversation meandered after that, and they didn't touch on anything too personal again. Sebastian opened another bottle of wine, and after doing the dishes and cleaning the kitchen together, they settled down in front of the TV. They both sat on the couch, their shoulders and legs touching.

"If I didn't know better I'd think you intended to seduce me," Jen said, feeling surprisingly comfortable.

"Because I've been plying you with alcohol?"

"Don't think I haven't noticed."

"I didn't force you to drink. For all I know you might intend to jump me." His eyes glowed with suppressed humor, his large frame more relaxed than normal. "What would you like to watch? Rom-com or action movie?"

"Action movie," she said.

Sebastian pushed a few buttons and placed his arm around her shoulders, drawing her nearer.

"Is that your best seduction move?"

"Nope. I was feeling cold."

Jen grinned. "Liar."

"Shush, the movie's starting."

Disinclined to move, she cuddled against him and concentrated on the movie. His scent wrapped around her while his warmth soaked into her side. Fully relaxed, physical tiredness claimed her. Her eyelids kept falling shut and finally she gave up the fight and slept.

As the closing credits of the movie started, Sebastian carefully separated himself from Jen and stood. She didn't wake when he picked her up and carried her down the passage to his room. After managing to pull back the covers with one hand, he set her down gently. She murmured something unintelligible when he removed her shoes, but still didn't wake. He was tempted to join her but didn't. Wayne wanted her, and he couldn't make a move on Jen or do anything that might upset Wayne.

Loving Wayne the way he did meant it wouldn't be fair of Sebastian to take his friendship with Jen any further. No, it would be best if he left her to sleep in his bed. Alone.

A quick glance at his watch confirmed the lateness of the hour. Wayne had obviously decided to stay the night with his parents. He'd spend the night in Wayne's bed. Wayne wouldn't mind.

Chapter Four

"SEBASTIAN!"

Sebastian grunted, rolling over to avoid another elbow to the ribs. "Damn it, Wayne." His voice was gritty with sleep, but he came awake quickly with a half-naked Wayne leaning over him. The darkness of the room made his other senses pop, and he could smell Wayne's aftershave and the soap they used in the shower. "Do you have to shake me?"

"Why are you in my bed? You have a perfectly good one in your room."

"Jen's using it. She stayed for dinner and went to sleep while we were watching a movie. It's cold. Put the covers back."

Wayne ignored his request. "Dude, why aren't you in there with her? You're missing a perfect chance to make a move on her."

"Not when I know you're interested in her."

"I told you last night. Both of us should go after her."

"For a little fun? I don't want fun." Sebastian squeezed his eyes shut at the pain knifing him in the chest. "I want a relationship with someone who cares for me. *Me.* Not the possessions I bring to the table."

"Shift over." Wayne slid onto the bed, and pulled the covers back into place.

Sebastian froze, his breath catching when Wayne pressed his cold body against his back. "Snuggling?"

Wayne chuckled, not embarrassed in the least. "You're warm. We could have something special with Jen. I don't know why I didn't think of it before."

"Man, I know you're the idea person in our business, but have you thought this through? Say we go ahead. You know some of what Fletch and Liam went through when they hooked up with Gaby. Do you want that for Jen? People abusing her in public? And what about your family? Surely they wouldn't approve?"

Wayne's adopted family was brilliant, but he didn't think they'd feel comfortable about Wayne sharing a woman. They held traditional values. Not that there was anything wrong with that.

Sebastian took a shallow breath and tried to ignore Wayne's solid chest at his back. "Besides, Jen and I discussed threesomes over dinner. We decided there was potential for pain. I don't want to lose your friendship."

"Don't be silly." Wayne's warm breath blew across his ear.

Gooseflesh pebbled on Sebastian's arms and legs. *Move your mouth a little lower.* Self-loathing followed swiftly, and he burst into speech. "All I'm saying is you can't just decide something like this. Not when it has the potential to blow up in our faces."

"Ah, so you are considering my suggestion."

"Jen intends to focus on her studies. Besides, there's one thing you haven't mentioned. What about you and me? We'll touch. Three sets of hands and mouths get confusing. Could you handle me kissing you? Getting that up close and personal?"

Bloody hell! He'd definitely drunk too much tonight. He hadn't meant to blurt out stuff like that.

There was a long pause and Sebastian's mouth twisted. Yeah, exactly what he'd thought. Introduce a little bit of gayness to the conversation and Wayne clearly hesitated.

"Do you think Fletch and Liam fuck each other?"

Sebastian grunted and rolled over to face Wayne. Not that he could see much in the dark. "That's none of our business, but they do seem comfortable together."

"Yeah, that's what I thought," Wayne said. "You'd better go back to your own bed. I'm sure Jen won't mind once you explain about the couch."

Disappointment surged through Sebastian. Of course. Once the conversation became difficult Wayne bailed. Not that he could blame him. Most other men would do the same. Without another word he rolled off the bed and left. His bed was a king. He could get some sleep and not even touch Jen.

Jen was asleep when he entered his bedroom. The soft snores were charming, although she probably wouldn't thank him for mentioning the fact. Gingerly, he climbed into his bed and replaced the covers. For summer it was still damn cold.

Just about as cold as Wayne's rejection.

Ah! He'd noticed Sebastian's weird behavior lately. His moodiness. Thick-head that he was, he'd thought Seb was working through his feelings about his divorce. But maybe it was something else entirely. He thought back over the time Sebastian had stayed with him, let his mind wander the possibilities given their conversation. The way Sebastian froze the instant he'd touched him.

Wayne knew Sebastian loved him. When Wayne had been adopted and Sebastian hadn't, they'd stayed friends at school and Wayne's adopted parents had let him invite Sebastian over to play most weekends. Yeah, the love wasn't in doubt, but what if it was more? And how the heck should he feel about it?

Wayne flopped over on his back and placed his hands under his head as an extra pillow.

Could he kiss Sebastian? Would he enjoy it?

Nah, he liked women. He liked their softness and the way they smelled. He liked their laughter and even their prickly moods. And he loved fucking them. Bottom line—he couldn't think of a world, his world, without a woman as a lover.

His mind darted from thought to thought, never settling or coming to a decision. The plain truth was he didn't know. The last thing he wanted was to screw up his close friendship with Sebastian, yet he could sense that would happen if he didn't handle his new knowledge carefully.

And Jen. He had no idea why he hadn't noticed her charms before. No, that wasn't quite true. He hadn't allowed himself to consider Jen in a romantic light before because she'd worked for them.

But now that problem no longer existed. A sense of rightness filled him as his mind drifted back. He couldn't get past the way Jen had felt in his arms when she'd pitched headlong into orgasm, and the glance he'd exchanged with Sebastian at the time. The connection that had clicked into place felt right. *Perfect.*

He blew out a gust of air, his lungs starting to burn before he inhaled again.

A plan—something to propel the three of them forward into the next stage. Let the cards fall where they may and all that crap. Yeah. His mouth curled into a sly smile as a plan formed in his mind. Audacious and daring, but it just might work...

JEN WOKE SLOWLY, AWARE of the heat at her back. A foreign warmth. The tick of a clock that wasn't normally there. Confusion slammed through her. Her eyes flicked open. Focused. The first thing she noticed was the bookcase, overflowing with books. Her mind sharpened, memories clicking into place. She turned over abruptly, her elbow connecting with hard flesh.

"Ow. Why does everyone attack my ribs? I'm turning black and blue."

"Why are we in bed together?" Her hand slid furtively beneath the covers. Whew. She was fully clothed, which meant...

Disappointment hit the instant her mind fixed on the truth. She was in bed with one of her hunky bosses and nothing had happened.

"Wayne came home and kicked me out of his bed."

"Did we drink a lot last night?"

"A few beers and some wine."

Huh. No wonder her mouth felt like the desert on a scorching hot day. She swallowed but it didn't make any difference. "I guess I should go home."

Sebastian squinted at his watch. "It's still early. I'll drop you off on the way to work."

"My neighbors will gossip."

"So? It's none of their business."

"You don't know my neighbors. They probably witnessed me punching Giles and have spread it all over Sloan."

"Giles got what was coming to him." His gaze angled her way. "If your neighbors cause you this much stress then maybe you should sell."

"Maybe."

"Where would you like to live, location-wise?"

"I haven't thought about it too hard." But Sebastian was right. She'd known the neighbors from the time she was old enough to speak. It was like having extra sets of parents looking out for her. Okay if she was seven, but not so much fun now that she was dating and old enough for sleepovers.

"Do I get a kiss good morning?"

His husky voice broke off her train of thought. "What?" While they stared at each other her heart tried to break out of her chest. "Why?"

"Because I didn't get a kiss good night?"

She huffed out a laugh. "Not a good enough reason. Besides, I have morning breath."

"Not a good enough reason." He lobbed her excuse back at her and shifted closer before she could blink. He lowered his head slowly, giving her an out if she wanted it. Jen didn't move a muscle. Their lips brushed, and Sebastian lifted his head.

"You call that a kiss?" she muttered in disgust.

A slow grin broke out, transforming his expression into one of mischief, and he pounced before she could react. There was nothing tentative about this kiss. Their lips fit together perfectly, his big hands cradling her head while he plundered her mouth. Sensations danced across her skin like tiny water sprites doing an erotic dance.

After a few seconds of his confident touch, she burned. Her clothes became cumbersome and heavy. Too restrictive when she wanted to rub against him like a cat. A purr of pleasure built in her chest and she clutched his shoulders, fighting for fuller contact. He sipped and tasted, stealing her air, making her dizzy.

When he finally lifted his head, his eyes glittered. "How is your hand today?"

She unclenched the hand that had—unbeknownst to her—found a place in his hair and frowned at it. "It feels fine. A bit stiff and achy but nothing too bad."

"I should have kissed you last night," he said.

"Yeah, right. Those magic lips would have done the trick."

His eyes twinkled. "I'd like to kiss you again."

"Ah, I don't think that's a good idea."

"Coward."

"I've just come out of a relationship. Starting another one—"

"Giles doesn't count. Look, I could use the same excuse, but couldn't we take things slow? Aw, fuck." He bit off the curse, suddenly looking a bit sick. "No, you're right. We can't do this."

"Why?" she demanded.

"Because Wayne likes you, and I don't intend to get into a dispute over any woman."

Jen led with her elbow, digging him in the ribs. "I'm not property."

A grunt escaped him and he shifted a fraction. "Sorry. I didn't mean that how it sounded."

She narrowed her eyes at him, letting him see her displeasure. "Shouldn't I have some say?"

Sebastian's head jerked up, his attention on a sound near the doorway.

"Can I join in the fun?" Wayne sauntered into the bedroom wearing nothing but a broad smile.

Jen's focus shot straight to his cock. "I notice you're happy to see us," she said drily.

"Jesus," Sebastian muttered. "Close your eyes and I'll get rid of him."

"And miss the free show? I don't think so." Jen's gaze slid down, taking in the muscles in Wayne's legs and calves before traveling upward again, past his narrow hips and erection to his broad chest. It was smooth and hair-free unlike Sebastian's. She'd felt his crisp chest hair when they'd kissed. Finally she studied the tribal tattoo that swirled over part of Wayne's left arm and shoulder. Sexy, and just perfect to lick.

"Damn, Wayne. Go and get some clothes."

"No, wait," she blurted. "Let me see your butt."

Sebastian groaned.

"What?" she asked. "I need to fuel my fantasies. Sex toys are no fun without the fantasy."

Grinning, Wayne did a model-like swivel and pranced around, letting her view his body from every conceivable angle. Then he strutted right up to the bed and sat down before rolling next to her. "Why settle for fantasies when you can have the real thing?"

Sebastian *tsked* under his breath. "Is that the normal spiel you give your girlfriends?"

Wayne waggled his eyebrows without taking his attention from her. "I work with the tools at hand. Do I get a kiss?"

Wayne moved before Jen could answer, sliding onto the bed and slanting his mouth over hers. A burst of mint danced across her taste buds, making her conscious of her morning breath. It didn't seem to bother Wayne. He held her close, twirling his tongue with hers until desire clawed at her. When he finally lifted his head to wink at her, she was breathing hard and was totally confused. How could she respond to both men? It hadn't even seemed weird knowing that Sebastian was watching them. If anything, Sebastian's presence had made her hotter.

Wayne propped himself up on his elbow and peered over at Sebastian. "Do I get a kiss from you too?"

Jen felt her eyes widen. A shocked sound came from Sebastian but it was cut off by Wayne. Without hesitation, one big hand cupped Sebastian's head. Jen watched, her mouth dropping open as the two men kissed. It was fierce. It was urgent and bruising, Sebastian resisting before the fight suddenly sapped from him. He groaned. Jen saw the kiss gentle and the weird tension seep away. When their lips finally parted, their gazes caught and held.

Curiosity ran rampant in her. Had they done this before? Then another thought bloomed and horror filled her. She'd kissed Sebastian. She didn't want to break up the two men if they were together in that way. She ripped her gaze off them, suddenly uncomfortable, wishing she were somewhere else instead of trapped between the two hard bodies like the filling in a sandwich. "Are you guys gay?"

"No."

"No!" Wayne echoed.

She scanned their expressions. Both men looked weird, a bit shocked.

Sebastian cleared his throat. "Ah, that was interesting."

Wayne, who normally had a lot to say for himself, remained silent. He moved a fraction, flipping back the covers to crawl into the bed next to her. The sandwich came to mind again. He pressed close and something hard poked her in the thigh. Good grief. He still had an erection. Curiouser and curiouser.

"Um, what time do you guys need to leave for work?"

"When we're ready," Wayne said.

Okay.

"I'll take you home after breakfast," Sebastian said.

"We'll pick you up for dinner at six," Wayne said.

Breakfast. Dinner? "Why?"

"Jen, think," Wayne said in a gentle rumble. "We're courting you."

"But..." She glanced at Sebastian, saw the watchfulness in his pale eyes. Her attention wandered to Wayne. "But..."

"We want you to come to dinner and spend time with us. If it will make you feel better we'll invite Gaby, Fletch and Liam too," Wayne said. "Gaby will help you keep us in line."

"Do you want to take a shower?" Sebastian asked. "I can give you some clothes to wear home."

"Ah, thanks." Clothes, dinner, dating. Things were moving way too quickly for her brain this morning. She couldn't think of a single reason to refuse. And if Gaby was there too... Maybe she could ask Gaby a few questions about how she and her men managed to interact together on a permanent basis without things turning weird. Her mouth dropped open. Cripes, was she actually considering climbing into bed with both of them?

Sebastian jumped out of bed and rummaged through a set of drawers. He produced a pair of board shorts and a pale blue T-shirt, silently handing them to her.

"There are clean towels in the bathroom cupboard," Wayne said.

Jen glanced at both of them again and nodded. Without warning she felt superfluous and accepted the clothes from Sebastian with a curt nod before making a rapid exit.

She scurried down the passage, entering the bathroom and locking the door with a loud click. Only then did she slump against the wall and attempt to even out her breathing.

Was she really going to do this? Wayne and Sebastian—both of them?

Sebastian waited until he heard the lock of the bathroom door slide home. *Excellent.* Jen wouldn't interrupt them for a few minutes.

"What the hell was that?" The words erupted from him, carrying every ounce of the confusion swirling around inside him.

"An experiment."

He paused, willing Wayne to expound. He didn't. Instead he stared at him, making Sebastian want to shuffle his feet. A reversion to his uncomfortable schoolboy days when he'd stood in front of the class and stammered like an idiot. The other kids had jeered him.

"I'll go and start the coffee." He took two steps toward the door.

"Coward."

Sebastian spun to glare at Wayne. "What do you want

from me? What do you want me to say? That we'll braid each other's hair?"

Wayne spluttered, the seriousness leaving his brown eyes. "Mate, you don't have enough hair to braid. But Jen has long enough hair for both of us to plait at the same time."

The *oomph* in Sebastian's argument popped. "Is this a good idea?"

"I don't know," Wayne said, sobering. "But I like Jen, and it felt right holding her while she climaxed. I liked sharing that with you."

"Just because it felt good that doesn't make it right."

"Of course not. All three of us need to be in agreement."

"And that's why you—" Sebastian gestured with his hand, unable to squeeze the words past the lump in his throat. *Wayne kissed me.*

"Kissed you. I figured you were right last night. I don't want to go into this with reservations. I might quiz Fletch and Liam tonight."

"I...you can't!"

"Why not? Didn't you like the kiss?"

"I'll go and put on the coffee. Jen will be finished in a moment." Sebastian fled, knowing it was cowardly but unable to stay a moment longer in his room when Wayne was in his bed.

Naked.

In the kitchen he realized the only item of clothing he wore was his boxer-briefs. God, between the two of them they'd scare Jen away before they'd even started. He took two steps down the passage before coming to an abrupt halt. Nope. He'd stay the way he was. He wasn't ashamed of his body but he was worried about his control. Christ, Wayne had flaunted himself, then leaned over to kiss him as if he did it every day.

Sebastian's stomach flipped, and he couldn't decide if it was fear or excitement. Messages of lust raced through his veins at the memory of Wayne's lips teasing his, the friction of morning stubble against his chin. He hadn't realized how sexy that would be, how the sandpaper sensation would fire his cock to life.

With a shaky hand he reached for the coffeepot. He managed to fill it with cold water despite the continuing tremors. Wayne had kissed him. *Wayne kissed Jen too.* Damn, why did his brain have to broadcast that particular thought?

But Wayne wouldn't play him.

That was one thing he knew without a doubt.

Footsteps heralded an arrival. Sebastian fought the urge to glance over his shoulder. Wayne— No! He forced himself to collect eggs from the pantry. Scrambled eggs and bacon. If he focused on cooking he might make it through the next hour until they left for work without doing anything stupid.

JEN LET THE WARM water pour down over her shoulders. She'd seen the wet room at Gaby's house but had never used one before. The wide, open spaces of the bathroom made her glad she'd locked the door, but she had to admit that not having to watch herself while stepping into the shower was excellent. Way less potential for stubbed toes. And she didn't have to worry about water splashes because that was what the bathroom was designed for with the waterproof tiles on the walls and floor. And the extra shower heads. She twisted a lever and water massaged her from a different angle. Pure decadence. The entire room was modern and sleek and she loved it. So much room.

Without warning her mind stepped out of line and flooded her with images of two men sharing the shower with her. Wet, naked limbs. Roving hands. Teasing mouths...

A husky groan slipped from her as arousal zipped the length of her body, settling between her thighs with an insistent hum. One hand crept up to cup her breast before she jerked it away in disgust. She didn't have time for romance or sex or any of the other emotions that came hand in hand with a man. *Men.*

She grabbed a face cloth and lathered it up with shower gel. A burst of citrus surrounded her, a tonic to her scattered senses. She briskly cleansed her body. Thinking about one man, let alone two, rated as plain stupidity.

She had a plan for the rest of her life and the next year didn't include any wild sex.

So there!

Her body didn't take the slightest bit of notice, ignoring her decision by softening and aching for a hard cock. Grumpily, she turned off the water and toweled herself dry. Five minutes later she padded down the passage to the kitchen, enticed by the scent of coffee and cooking bacon. The borrowed clothes rubbed against her skin as she entered the kitchen. She tugged at them and furiously averted her mind from everything related to sex.

Wayne sat at the breakfast counter, reading the local paper while Sebastian was busy cooking.

Wayne looked up at her arrival. His brown eyes studied her warmly, his slow smile making her clothes start to itch again. "Would you like coffee?"

She shuffled her feet, trying to get comfortable. "Thanks."

"Black?"

"A little milk, please." So polite. With her pulse racing, she selected one of the other stools at the breakfast counter and perched.

"What are you going to do today?" Wayne asked, placing a mug of coffee in front of her.

Glad of something to do, she seized the coffee and took a cautious sip.

"How's the hand?" Sebastian asked, his gaze settling for an instant before returning to the pan in front of him.

"What did you do to your hand?"

Sebastian set plates in front of both of them. "She punched Giles in the nose."

"I'm not sorry," she mumbled, her cheeks heating with embarrassment. Even though her hand still throbbed, she'd do it again.

"He deserved it," Sebastian said. "I wanted to hit him but she wouldn't let me."

Wayne smirked. "Giles had it coming. I wish I'd been there."

"He'll probably press charges," Jen said.

"You forget I was a witness." Sebastian grabbed the third plate and the last remaining stool. "He's probably too embarrassed to tell anyone what really happened."

"Your day sounds more exciting than mine. I played

rugby with the relations and ate lunch. If Giles causes any trouble let us know. Okay?"

Jen nodded even though she didn't mean it. She was an adult and more than capable of taking care of herself.

"I see Ms. Knowall has a column in the paper," Wayne said.

Sebastian snorted. "Who is she darting with her poisonous pen this week?"

"Evidently the Children of Nature Cult is in disarray. Some of their women of marriageable age are refusing to marry within the cult. And there's mention of new products coming from Fancy Free in time for Valentine's Day."

Jen took a sip of coffee. "Does anyone know who is writing the column these days? It was Gaby's sister, but she promised not to write another column after the debacle with Gaby at the supermarket."

"We'll have to quiz Gaby tonight." Wayne whipped his cell phone out of his pocket and hit speed dial. After a brief conversation with Fletch, he hung up. "Fletch said he'd check with Gaby and Liam, but he thought they could make it."

"Do you want me to make a dessert?" Jen asked.

"Sounds good," Sebastian said.

Gradually some of the tension lifted from her. Wayne

and Sebastian were nice. Spending time with them wouldn't be a hardship, especially with Gaby to help bolster her nerves.

Chapter Five

THIS BARBEQUE HAD BEEN a bad idea. Gaby had been sending her speculative looks ever since she, Fletch and Liam had arrived. So far she hadn't managed to get Jen alone to quiz her. Judging by Gaby's determined demeanor it wouldn't be long until she faced an inquisition.

"I put my house on the market today." As far as diversions went this was a good one.

"What?" Wayne asked.

"Why?" Gaby demanded.

Sebastian just stared at her, flanked by Liam and Fletch who appeared equally interested.

"It's too big for one person." Jen squared her shoulders. "The house needs a family."

"But what will you do? Where will you go?" Gaby asked.

"I'll buy an apartment or something smaller eventually.

The real estate market is flat at present. The agent said sales are slow in Sloan, and it might take a long time, but selling makes sense."

"And now?" Wayne asked.

"I'll look for a suitable flat, not far from school."

"Anyone want another drink?" Sebastian asked.

"I like this song," Fletch said. "Dance with me." He grabbed Liam and yanked him into his arms, smooching as he started to dance. Liam laughed and relaxed against Fletch, his lips grazing Fletch's cheek. They murmured in undertones, clearly at ease with each other.

Jen stared, their intimacy reminding her of that morning when Wayne and Sebastian had kissed.

"Don't gawk," Gaby said.

"They look happy." Jen had seen them interact before, but this time seemed different. Not that she thought any less of the two men. It was kinda sexy, and she was flattered that they liked her enough to feel comfortable. Both men were equally affectionate and demonstrative with Gaby.

A masculine arm slipped around her shoulders. "Feeling left out, Jen?" Sebastian whispered, his breath warm against her ear. "Come and dance with me."

Jen found herself slow-dancing with Sebastian out on the deck. "Do you think any of them feel left out?"

"I don't know. Ask Gaby," Sebastian said.

Something in his voice made her move back so she could see his face. "Are you okay?"

"Confused." Chagrin chased across his face at the admission.

Jen glanced around, head turning, gaze darting, but no ready answer pounced out at her. "You and me both. I feel as if I'm on a rollercoaster without a safety belt. I don't like it."

"You can always get off."

Jen sucked in a hasty breath, giving a slight shake of her head. This was so new, but she'd regret fleeing from Wayne and Sebastian. She just knew it. "I don't think I can."

"This situation scares you."

"Doesn't it worry you?"

"Hell yeah." Sebastian's grasp tightened on her shoulders, his face displaying the same turmoil that traversed her mind. "I'm taking each day one at a time. I hate the out-of-control feeling."

Jen nodded, a wave of sympathy filling her. She understood the off-balance sensation. Heck, she was living it right along with him.

The song ended and another took its place.

"My turn," Wayne said.

Jen stepped away from Sebastian and turned expectantly to Wayne. Wayne winked at her and put his arms around

Sebastian.

"Right, that does it. We're going to talk." Gaby grabbed Jen's arm and dragged her inside into the kitchen. "What's going on with you guys?"

"Nothing," Jen said, going with the truth because it was easier. "I spent the night here last night."

"*Nada?*" Gaby almost screeched. "You're telling me I'm imagining things?"

"I hurt my hand. Sebastian drove me to the doctor."

"Old news. My mother rang me this morning wanting deets."

Jen blinked in shock even though she was aware of the gossip vine in Sloan. "Everyone knows?"

"Yeah, well fight out in the street and that's what happens," Gaby said, waving it off as inconsequential. "Although from what I hear, Giles deserved it." She paused, her eyes widening. "You're not going to distract me. If nothing happened then why are you here tonight?"

Jen frowned. "They asked me, and I said yes."

"And what are you going to do next?"

"Refuse to answer nosy questions. It's not as if I know the answers anyway. What's the story about the new sex toy coming out? The one the cult is protesting about."

"Top secret," Gaby said, tapping the side of her nose with her forefinger. "I could do with someone to test out the design I'm working on at present though."

"A vibrator?"

"Of sorts," Gaby said with a laugh.

"What does that mean?"

"It's a vibrating butt plug."

"I guess I could try that."

"Your men might like it too." Gaby's black curls danced as she laughed. "Liam and Fletch do. I'll drop it off after work tomorrow."

"What are you doing?" Sebastian demanded in an undertone.

Definitely testy. Wayne bit back a grin. "Going with my gut instinct."

"Which is to flirt with me? You're lucky I didn't punch you in the nose."

Yep, now was not the time to smirk. Wayne moved in time to the music, not much more than a sway really. Dancing with Sebastian was fun. Fletch and Liam hadn't reacted with anything other than grins, and after the initial shock Sebastian had gradually relaxed in his embrace.

"Don't be silly. You want me." Aw, hell. *Blabbermouth.* This wasn't the best time to force this conversation. He sure as hell didn't want to give Sebastian a chance to run. But having their friends around acted as a kind of a buffer.

At least for this initial conversation.

"I'm sorry." Sebastian's throat worked in a swallow, his shoulders hunching, and Wayne could see the fear in his friend, the shame.

"No!" Fuck he didn't want to make Sebastian uncomfortable or to make him think he should run. "Don't apologize. It doesn't scare me." His fingers bit into Seb's biceps. "This doesn't scare me."

Sebastian checked the whereabouts of the others before leaning closer. "You're not worried about the fact that I want to touch your cock?"

"I liked kissing you this morning. Besides, I've seen your cock. There's nothing scary about it."

"Yeah, well." Sebastian averted his gaze, and Wayne noticed a tinge of pink creeping into his cheeks. "What about your family? What will they think?"

"It's none of their business. I've told you that." Wayne hesitated, then decided to spit out the question uppermost in his mind. "Have you had sex with a guy before?"

A choking sound came from Sebastian, and Wayne widened the distance between them to scan Sebastian's expression. A whole raft of emotions flickered for him to see, not that he could understand shit.

Sebastian's mouth worked but there was no sound.

"Seb?"

"Jesus, no!" Sebastian snapped.

"So it's only me you want."

"Stop making fun of me."

"I'm not. Look we'll talk later tonight when everyone has gone. Just you and me."

Sebastian shrugged without looking at him. "Whatever. I thought you'd want me to leave."

"You're not going anywhere." Wayne grinned, feeling good about the decision. "So, it's a date."

"*It's not a date.*"

"Yes it is. We can even have a drink, but don't think you're gonna get lucky. I don't put out on the first date."

"Jesus," Sebastian muttered. "I need a drink." He pulled away and stomped off, leaving Wayne standing alone. A slow grin broke free. This dating business could be fun.

During the rest of the evening Sebastian waited for smart-arse comments from Fletch and Liam. They didn't come, not one of their friends passing judgment or even commenting.

Sebastian fought the trepidation stalking him, the anxiety that settled on his shoulders like a heavy bag of cement. He didn't know what Wayne wanted from him, was worried about what it might mean.

Gaby, Fletch and Liam left just after eleven, taking Jen

with them.

Sebastian frowned after the tail lights of the departing vehicle. "I could have dropped Jen at her place."

"I didn't want to give you the opportunity to duck out on me. You've looked petrified every time I caught your gaze."

"I am," Sebastian mumbled, frightened to even look at Wayne.

"You want another drink?"

"Nah, we need to be on the job site at six tomorrow morning. I don't want to do it with a hangover."

"Let's go to bed then."

"Together?" Damn, his voice had squeaked like a teenager's. He scuffed one bare foot over a black mark on the tiles. It didn't shift.

"I want to kiss you again. Come on." Wayne grabbed his hand and towed Sebastian from the kitchen, turning off lights as they went. He dragged Sebastian into his room, his bare feet noiseless on the tiled floor.

"What are we doing?"

"We're getting comfortable with each other because I want to know if my hard-on this morning was a one-off."

"You'd just kissed Jen."

Wayne started to unbutton Sebastian's shirt. Sebastian's heart attempted to escape his chest, battering his ribs with hard knocks and the accompanying sharp pain reminded him to breathe.

"Don't you worry," Wayne said. "I'm clear about what I want from Jen. You like her, right?"

"Jen's amazing. Not many women her age would give up so much to look after their mother."

"See. Jen's not the problem. We need to sort out whatever is going on with us. I'm done talking." Wayne ran his palm across Sebastian's chest. The calluses from his years of doing manual work dragged across Sebastian's pectoral muscles, pulled at his nipples. A moan spilled from his parted lips and he shivered at the illicit pleasure skittering through him. Wayne slipped the shirt off Sebastian's shoulders and tossed it aside. Rough fingers unfastened his belt and tugged at the zipper of his jeans.

And Sebastian let him.

All the time Wayne watched him closely until Sebastian felt like one of their new building apprentices on their first day of the job.

Sebastian's breaths seesawed from his lungs, harsh and loud. Finally self-preservation made him jerk from Wayne's touch. "What are you doing? You're starting to make me feel uncomfortable."

"Not awkward enough to leave my room," Wayne said with a trace of smugness.

"Smart-arse." Sebastian bit back a verbal reaction when Wayne's fingers skimmed his cock as he lowered the zipper. Even through the layer of denim and his boxer-briefs, it felt intimate. Too much. *Not enough.* Wayne tugged his jeans down his hips and urged him to step out of them.

"Do you want to keep your underwear?"

Sebastian hesitated. It wasn't as if his boxers were doing a good job of hiding his growing erection.

"Executive decision," Wayne said, and before Sebastian could react, his friend whisked them down his legs. "On the bed. You can get under the covers if you want."

Sebastian followed the orders blindly, even as he silently debated the wisdom of remaining in his friend's bedroom.

In his bed.

Naked.

He watched Wayne undress and didn't sense any of the nerves that he, himself, struggled with. Wayne always made his decisions quickly and once he'd made one, he never swerved from his goal. Never second-guessed his actions. He'd always been the same, for as long as Sebastian had known him.

The sheets and duvet smelled like Wayne, and if anything the familiar scent ramped up his stress levels. Though try telling his dick this was wrong. Maybe that was why he was feeling so lightheaded. All the blood that normally helped his mind to function had zapped south for a fiesta.

Wayne strutted to the bed. While he didn't have a full-blown erection like Sebastian, he was getting there. Sebastian swallowed in an attempt to lubricate his mouth and throat.

"You look like a cowering rabbit about to get jumped by a predator."

Sebastian huffed out a harsh breath. "Not far wrong."

"All I'm doing is taking your idea and running with it."

"Because you want to or because you want to placate me?" Sebastian's sharp tone cut through the air, charging the atmosphere yet again, changing it to something prickly and explosive.

"Seb, you have to decide if you trust me or not. I can't make up your mind for you."

"That's true."

"You've been thinking about this for a while."

"Yeah."

"All I want to do is kiss, touch and sleep together in the same bed for the rest of the night. There's nothing daunting about that."

Sebastian gulped as Wayne climbed onto the bed and arranged the duvet over his lower body. They stared at each other and moved at the same time. Hands grasped shoulders. Flesh met flesh and lips joined in a kiss. It was a hesitant yet surprisingly sensual kiss, the caution lighting a slow flame within Sebastian.

Wayne squirmed closer. Heck Sebastian couldn't argue with that. The urge to plaster himself against Wayne gripped him. Might as well go for broke. He pushed past his caution, deepening the tentative kiss, rimming Wayne's mouth with his tongue. With his actions, he silently requested Wayne to give way and open to him. Wayne moaned and suddenly they were touching from mouth to knee. Their cocks brushed.

Pleasure grabbed Sebastian by the scruff of the neck. Too much yet not enough. His tongue dueled with Wayne's. A hard, muscular chest rubbed against his. Wayne pulled away, breathing hard. Sebastian grew rigid, suspecting that Wayne intended to shove him away.

Too much. Too fast.

But instead Wayne trailed kisses down Sebastian's neck. He sucked a couple of bites of the tender skin, jolting Sebastian to the core.

"Damn, that feels good." The combination of raspy stubble and the hard draw of a mouth did things to his dick. Sebastian's hips jerked, sliding their cocks together.

Uneasy, he wondered what Wayne was thinking, because he wasn't saying a word. Was he horrified? He wasn't acting that way. Going on instinct, he ground his cock against Wayne's, no longer pretending it was an accident. If Wayne was gonna freeze because of a little cock action then Sebastian needed to know now before he invested his heart.

"Damn," Wayne whispered. "Do that again."

Not the reaction he'd expected. Sebastian repeated the grinding motion, frustrated that it wasn't enough. While it felt good, the friction exasperated him. He needed more.

"Hell. Let me." Wayne shifted a fraction and grabbed Sebastian's cock. He curled his fingers around his shaft too and started to pump. Up and down. Up and down.

Sebastian closed his eyes and blindly sought Wayne's mouth. The hard strokes were exactly what he liked and never got from a woman. Pre-cum soon moistened the grasp of Wayne's hand. Sebastian wasn't sure if it came from him or Wayne but didn't spend too much time pondering the question. Instead he continued to kiss Wayne, softening his mouth and taking the kisses into lazy and sensual.

Wayne's fingers tightened around their shafts, the contrast of hard and soft driving Sebastian to distraction. His balls drew tight, the electric feeling of orgasm zapping him past the point of no return.

Gradually he drifted back to Earth. He blinked slowly

and fixed his gaze on a spot somewhere over the tattoo on Wayne's shoulder. Hell, what had he done? What if Wayne ended up hating him?

"Seb?"

Sebastian had to clear his throat to make way for speech. He coughed a second time while his mind frantically tried to plan what he should say. "Yeah?" *Real smooth!*

Wayne climbed off the bed and nailed him with a glare. "Wait there."

Not quite what he was expecting. Every muscle in his body tensed as he stared after his friend. Gradually he became aware of the cum painted over his belly and shame crept into the fringes of his mind. His weird yearning for Wayne would start their friendship rotting. How could it not? Wayne's family loved him, and they'd blame Sebastian if gossip started to spread around Sloan.

"Stop!" Wayne had returned and stood by the bed. "I can feel your mind working overtime. It was what it was. Sex between two males. Deal with it and decide what you want to do next."

The harsh tone of Wayne's voice made Sebastian's stomach clench. "I'm sorry."

Wayne punched him in the arm.

"Ow! What did you hit me for?"

"Your brain needs resetting," Wayne snapped. "I want to

explore this with you, dammit. We don't have to go around holding hands, but I enjoyed the hell out of that jerk-off. I like kissing you, and I want to sleep in this bed with you tonight. Don't act like a girl and go all weird on me." He slapped a face cloth on Sebastian's stomach. "Clean up."

Sebastian caught the cloth before it dropped onto the sheets and rubbed away the stickiness. Suddenly everything settled in him, his equilibrium returning to level. He dropped the cloth on the floor to pick up later. "If your other dates go weird then you must be doing something wrong."

"Dick." Wayne slid back under the covers. He wrapped his arms around Sebastian. "What are we going to do about the Maxwell quote? Can we fit the job in before the end of February?"

The residual tension in Sebastian faded at Wayne's cool acceptance of the change in their relationship. He thought over the jobs they had lined up, considered the available crew. "We could put the new wet room in for them, but the kitchen project would need to wait until April. Unless we hire more crew. What do you think?"

"My stepbrothers are looking for work during the weekends."

"They'd need to commit. We can't have them ditching us to go out with their mates."

Wayne smiled and pressed a kiss to the curve of Sebastian's shoulder. "They'd listen to you. Mum thinks they're old enough to accept the responsibility."

Sebastian resettled his body, deliberately crowding Wayne. A part of him was surprised at the situation he found himself in, even though it was something he'd thought of for months. Wayne didn't shy from the contact, and warmth wove through Sebastian. "We could take them on for a trial period. Tell them to come and see me before school starts."

"It's better if you're in charge of them. They never listen to a word I say."

"Because you play the doting big brother and they twist you around their little fingers." His words forced another truth on him. Wayne loved his adopted family, his parents and his siblings. He wasn't sure how they'd react if they realized the depths of Wayne's intimacy with him. The burst of realism stayed with him for much of the night.

HER BED FELT LIKE a solitary island. Really lonely. Jen turned onto her side and wriggled to find a comfortable spot. How could this happen after one night? She'd hated sleeping the entire night in bed with Giles. In fact she'd never spent the night with her very first lover either.

When sleep remained elusive, she switched on the bedside lamp and picked up the list she'd started after Gaby had dropped her off.

The things she needed to do this week. There had been a message from the real estate agent on her answer phone. She was bringing a prospective buyer to view the house in the morning. Could Jen make sure the kitchen was clean, and if possible, put out some flowers? Maybe put on a pot of coffee or bake a cake to make the house smell inviting?

If the house sold she'd need to get rid of some of the furniture. Unless the prospective buyer wanted to purchase the contents from her. Jen jotted a note to remember to ask the real estate agent.

Her mind drifted to Wayne and Sebastian. *Heck, tell the truth.* She hadn't stopped thinking about them all day. A sense of excitement filled her every time her mind detoured to them, and she knew she'd decided to go ahead and explore where Wayne's crazy idea took them.

Gaby managed her two men, and they were happy. Jen might have harbored doubts at first and worried about Gaby, but her fears had proved groundless. It *was* possible to enjoy a healthy relationship with two men at the same time. All the threesome needed was open communication and trust. The willingness to compromise if necessary.

Funnily enough, trust wasn't an issue for her. She'd worked for Wayne and Sebastian full-time ever since her mother had died, and before that she'd had a part time job with them. Both men possessed integrity and honesty. No, it was the practicalities that scared her most.

What exactly were the logistics when it came to three lovers in a bed?

Or maybe she was overthinking the situation.

When the clock in the lounge struck six, Jen decided she might as well give up trying to sleep and plunge into her day. But at least she'd come to a decision. She'd ring either Wayne or Sebastian later today and invite herself for dinner. If she gave a broad enough hint they might even invite her for a sleepover.

Chapter Six

"THEY WANT TO BUY your house." Excitement glittered in the real estate agent's eyes, highlighting her model-perfect appearance. Immaculate blonde curls, a form-fitting black suit and high-heel red shoes showcasing long, slender legs screamed sex appeal. When combined with her calm efficiency she was guaranteed success in her chosen field. "At your asking price."

"But you said we'd probably have to drop the price and the buyers would come to me with offers." Jen didn't have to pretend bewilderment.

"They liked your house from the moment they walked in the door. They've been looking for the last year. And, they're cash buyers, so the only condition on the sale and purchase agreement is the requirement for the house to pass a building inspection. They're so keen they've already lined up a friend to inspect the building for them."

A knock on the front door interrupted the agent's enthusiasm. Jen's head was spinning, her thoughts a riot of emotions, the uppermost being what the heck had she done? She found herself at the door without even remembering walking from the kitchen where she'd been making a pot of coffee.

She inhaled a deep breath and opened the door.

"Liam? Has something happened to Gaby?"

"I'm here to inspect your house for Gary Seymour. I thought you'd only just listed your property."

"Yesterday," she said faintly. "I thought I'd have months to get used to the idea."

Liam squeezed her shoulder in a sympathetic manner. "This is a big house for one person. Your mother wouldn't want you to struggle to look after it."

Jen nodded, knowing he spoke the truth. But there were so many memories, both good and bad. She'd be leaving them behind. "Where do you want to start?"

"Inside, I think." He bent to unlace his boots and set them on the mat.

"You know the way." Jen left him to his task and returned to the kitchen. "That was Liam. He's come to do the inspection."

"I told you the buyers were keen. Would you like to sign the agreement now?"

"When do they want to take possession?"

"As soon as possible. My buyer asked if next Friday would work for you."

"That's not long!" Jen wanted to say no. She wanted to shove both the agent and Liam out of her house and pretend this had never happened. Then she thought of Gary Seymour. He had a family—three boys and a girl from memory. She thought of her mother and finally nodded. "Okay."

"Excellent."

The agent took her through the paperwork and after reading everything she signed the agreement, albeit with a shaky hand.

Liam finished his inspection and left. The agent departed not long afterward, leaving Jen alone with her shock. She had so much to do. Where was she going to live?

Her mind darted to Wayne and Sebastian. She'd talk to one of them. On automatic pilot she reached for the phone and rang the office. "Hi, Libby. It's Jen. Do you know where Wayne and Sebastian are this morning?"

"They're working out at the Portman property, but they have the council inspector there this morning."

Best she didn't interrupt them. "Can you ask them to ring me when they check in?"

"Sure thing, Jen," Libby said. "Oops, there's the other

line. I'll talk to you later."

Jen hung up and wondered where to start. She needed to pack her personal possessions, organize storage for the furniture she wanted to keep and find somewhere else to live. No problem. She could get that done in the allotted time.

Her morning passed in a blur of business. She organized to pick up cardboard cartons from the supermarket and started packing her clothes in the suitcases she'd unearthed from the attic. Her precious mementos were next, wrapped carefully in newspaper and packed in another suitcase. She picked up a photo of her and her mother, the last one they'd had taken together before her mother had become bedridden. Tears filled her eyes as she stared at her mother's smiling face.

"Jen!" A familiar masculine voice hollered through the house.

"Wayne, I'm up here in the bedroom."

"Right where we want you," Wayne said from the doorway.

"Don't tell her that, numbskull. You'll scare her."

Wayne stepped inside her bedroom, followed by Sebastian.

"What's wrong?" Sebastian scanned the cases and the mess on top of her bed. "Are you going somewhere?"

"A phone call would have done," she said faintly. With the two men in her bedroom it seemed to have shrunk.

"We had to come into town to do a couple of quotes," Sebastian said.

"And we figured we might score a kiss," Wayne added as he lifted her to her feet. Seconds later his mouth descended on hers, stealing her breath.

"My turn." Sebastian batted Wayne away and rubbed his forehead against hers. "You okay?"

"I feel a bit dazed. I've sold the house and have to move out in less than two weeks."

Instead of kissing her mouth, Sebastian kissed the tip of her nose in a teasing manner and released her. She stared, a little bemused. She'd never pictured him as playful. He was the serious one while Wayne joked around all the time. This was different. Despite the dark shadows under his eyes, he looked...content.

"Where are you going to move to?" Wayne asked.

"I don't know. I figured I'd check the flatmates wanted section of the local paper and see what I could find."

Wayne and Sebastian exchanged a glance then looked at her.

"Move in with us," Wayne said.

A *whoosh* of heat hit her, stealing her thoughts. Her mouth opened but not a sound emerged. She swallowed and tried again. "No, that's not a good idea. I'm not ready—"

"There's another spare room. We've been using it as a gym but it's no trouble to reorganize things. Sebastian and I both like you. We want to help out," Wayne said.

"We want you," Sebastian added. "But we'd never pressure you. You know that, right?"

Jen stared at them, noted their earnest expressions and finally nodded. "Okay. We all sleep in our own rooms."

Wayne grinned. "Sebastian and I have started sharing 'cause it gets lonely in the middle of the night."

Jen's gaze whipped to Sebastian. The tips of his ears turned pink as she watched.

"*Wayne.*"

"She'll work it out sooner or later. It's better to be up front with Jen. You'd prefer honest, eh?"

"Honesty is good. How big is my room? How much furniture will I be able to fit in it?"

"It's a fraction bigger than my room," Sebastian said.

"You looked around Sebastian's room? I'm jealous," Wayne said, putting on a pout.

"You know she's seen my room. Remember? We had torrid, hot sex," Sebastian said. "Before you came to join us."

"Oh, yeah." Wayne winked at her. "Couldn't have been

that good. She got dressed straightaway."

"No parading around naked," Jen said, putting on a stern face.

Both men grinned.

"Or in your underwear." After all, a girl could only handle so much. "Maybe this is a bad idea."

"Jen, you can trust us," Sebastian said. "We'd never force you into anything you weren't comfortable with, but we do like you. A lot."

"We might try to seduce you every Tuesday," Wayne added.

Sebastian checked his watch. "We'd better go or we'll be late. We'll come around after work and help you with packing. Maybe we could move some of the furniture and stuff tonight too."

"Thanks. That would be great." Her panic faded now that she had a plan.

Both Wayne and Sebastian planted a swift kiss on her lips and left. She stared at the open doorway, her fingers tracing her tingling lips, and all she could think was that she wished it were Tuesday.

The hours passed rapidly. Gaby arrived just after five, demanding details because Liam had been useless with the important info. After filling Gaby in on her plans, her friend was full of smirks.

"Wayne and Sebastian are perfect for you. You've known them for ages."

"But I'm nothing like the women they usually date," Jen said, picturing the leggy, stick-thin women she'd seen them with in the past.

"All men go through that phase. You should have seen some of the women Liam and Fletch dated. Just take things slowly and do what seems right."

"I want to jump them. The only problem is deciding which one to jump first," Jen said in a glum voice. "My mother is probably stirring in her grave at my wicked thoughts."

"That does it. I'm signing you on as an official tester. The pay isn't much, but it might help with your book costs."

"I forgot to ask Wayne what he wants me to pay for rent. What if I can't afford to stay with them? I still have to budget to make my money last until I complete my degree. I mean, I can't spend it all."

"Stop being stupid. Pull your weight around the house and pay a share of the bills. That's all you need to do. Somehow I don't think Wayne thinks of you as a tenant. I'll collect a tester kit for you tomorrow. All you need to do is sign a disclaimer and a privacy statement and you're good. Wayne and Sebastian will need to sign one too if you decide to recruit them to help you. I'll add them to the disclaimer statement."

"Whatever. Gaby, can you help me clean out Mum's room? I haven't done much more than dust and vacuum in there since Mum died."

"All you need to do is ask," Gaby said. "Why don't you have a garage sale? I'm sure the money will come in handy. I'll help you. Alice might be willing to lend a hand too," Gaby said, mentioning her boss.

Wayne and Sebastian arrived at six and Liam and Fletch turned up not long after. Despite her protests, Wayne and Sebastian loaded her bed and the other furniture she'd decided to keep onto the back of the truck they used for delivering supplies to sites.

"Don't be silly," Gaby said. "You might as well move now because it will make it easier to clean in here."

At eight, they stopped for the night and ate the pizza Jen had ordered. At nine thirty everyone left. Jen attempted to take her car, but Wayne hustled her into the truck and the three of them drove home together.

Home.

Although it was weird, the thought felt comfortable already. Exhausted from the physical activity, she helped unload the last of the boxes off the truck, made up her bed with clean sheets, had a shower and fell into bed.

A foreign scratching on the window woke her. She froze, the small hairs on the back of her neck prickling. When the fingernail-on-blackboard sound came again, she leapt out of bed and found herself halfway down the passage. She peeked into Sebastian's room. Empty. Stumbling a few more steps, she peered inside and made out two lumps on the bed.

"Wayne," she whispered.

"What is it?" Sebastian asked in a rumbly voice.

"A noise scared the crap out of me."

"Jen?

She'd woken Wayne as well. Feeling a bit stupid, she gnawed on her bottom lip, shifting her weight from foot to foot in indecision.

Wayne reached over to turn on the light and sat up in bed. "What are you doing here in the middle of the night?"

The sheets puddled in his lap, highlighting his naked chest and sexy tattoo. Sebastian rubbed his eyes, and she noticed his torso was naked too. He had a little chest hair and she immediately wanted to stroke him.

"Jen?" Wayne prompted.

Jen stared, overtaken by a sudden yearning to be in the middle of the bed between the two hard bodies. "I couldn't sleep in a strange room. It's Tuesday," she blurted.

Wayne bit back his need to chuckle. She'd remembered his Tuesday seduction rule and clearly wished she hadn't blabbed it out. She looked so cute with her long, curly hair hanging down around her shoulders and the thin purple nightgown skimming her body. As she moved self-consciously, her brown curls bounced and shifted, giving him a peek-a-boo show of her breasts. His heart twisted, a warm sensation gripping him.

Seb moved away from him and crawled out of bed. He crossed the distance to where Jen stood and ran the back of his hand over her cheek in a tender gesture. That one action brought the rightness of this strange situation to Wayne. He watched Seb grasp Jen's hand and tug her toward the bed. With gentle hands, he guided her down and slid in beside her.

"Turn off the light," he said once he'd settled. "I'm tired."

Wayne switched it off. At first Jen held her body tense, but gradually she relaxed. He could smell the scent of soap and clean woman and his cock perked up a little. *Not yet.* This was a delicate situation and he needed to handle it carefully. He'd take his cues from Jen. Seb was a little easier to read because they'd known each other for so long, but he'd take things slowly with Seb too. While he loved to have sex with a woman, he'd enjoyed his experiments with Seb. It had taken him a long time, but now he understood. Seb needed him, and he needed Seb. Together they were a balanced team.

"Want to fool around a little?" he whispered in Jen's ear. "We'll have to be quiet because Sebastian gets grumpy if he misses his sleep."

"I...maybe I should go back to my own room," she said in a rush.

"Stay. We won't do anything you're not comfortable with. I promise." His assurances seemed to soothe her apprehension. Wooing Sebastian and Jen might take a little juggling, but he was up to the challenge. Even if it had taken him ages to work it out. "Can I kiss you?"

"Not something I'd ever thought I'd hear my boss say."

"I'm not your boss now." The slot of lover was up for grabs.

She gave a breathless laugh. "It's going to take me time to remember."

"Let me give you something to help you," he murmured and claimed her lips before she had a chance to reply. Her scent and taste filled his senses, the bite of her fingers on his biceps letting him know this wasn't merely a pleasant dream. Giving in to temptation he let his hands wander, swallowing her gasp when he cupped one breast. It was full and soft, her nipple hardening rapidly at his touch. He slid the fabric back and forth across the taut peak, taking his time while he deepened the kiss.

The journey into arousal wasn't as fast as it had been with Seb. Instead it was different. Slow. Tender. He lifted his mouth and trailed it across her jaw. He nuzzled her neck, took in the way she leaned to give him better access and contentment settled on his shoulders.

"I want to taste you. Will you let me?" Asking permission seemed the thing to do, because he didn't want to take anything for granted at this early stage.

She hesitated, and he wished he could see her better in the dark.

"Jen?"

"Yes?"

"Will you let me take off your nightie?"

"Yes."

He didn't give her an opportunity to change her mind. He fumbled for the hem and drew the silky fabric up toward her head. She helped him, shifting her body weight. His fingers walked along the band of her panties. Her skin was smooth, making him wonder if she were that soft everywhere.

"Can I take your panties off too?"

"Depends. What do you want to do to me?" she

whispered, her breath warm against his neck.

Simple. "Everything. I'll settle for touching and tasting."

He half expected an argument, but Jen wriggled out of her panties and settled back against him. Yeah, she was yielding and fragrant everywhere.

His mouth wandered down her neck again. He licked her collarbone and nibbled a little, smiling at her *eep* of shock. He took his time, enjoying her sighs and the way she gradually relaxed, enjoying the low-level buzz of pleasure sliding through his own body. He licked across the curve of one breast and worried the nipple with his tongue.

"Wayne," she whispered and she clutched him to her, drawing him closer and giving a low cry of pleasure when he sucked strongly. Beside them Sebastian stirred but didn't wake. Jen froze again, as if she'd suddenly realized it wasn't just the two of them.

"Steady," he soothed. Time to give her something else to think about. He traveled down her body, touching and licking his way down her torso. He slipped lower in the bed, parted her legs and inserted himself into the space he'd created. His tongue lapped along the crease from hip to upper thigh, the scent of her arousal washing over him.

"Wayne, I don't think—"

"Don't think," he whispered and settled in to feast. Her flavor exploded on his tongue, tart and fragrant. He took his time exploring, learning what she enjoyed most. It was easy to tell because her fingers had slipped into his hair, and they tightened every time he licked closer to her clit. Flickers of his tongue drew throaty moans from her and direct stimulation made her tremble. Unable to resist, he pushed one finger inside her, the moist heat making him wish it was his cock instead. Shortly, he promised himself. When she was comfortable with them, with this situation.

Yeah, soon.

Jen gasped when he curved his finger. Ah, reading his stepsister's magazines hadn't been a waste of time. He circled her swollen clit with his tongue and continued his internal stimulation, listening for each catch of Jen's breath. Another lick. A moan escaped her, and then she was flying, her pussy clenching his finger with each hard spasm.

Wayne let her ride out the climax before moving up the bed again. He kissed her tenderly and drew her into his arms. "Can you sleep now?"

"I think so. What about you?" She sounded dazed, which filled him with smugness.

"Don't worry about me. Go to sleep."

Gradually she relaxed in his arms, and he let his thoughts drift, more content than he'd been for a long time. Not even his hard-on and tight balls put a dent in his satisfaction.

Sebastian wasn't sure how it had happened but waking up in bed with both Jen and Wayne started his day with a bang.

He leaned closer and whispered in Jen's ear. "You awake?"

"Leave her to sleep," Wayne said. "Let's talk in the kitchen."

Sebastian's gut bucked at the tone of Wayne's voice. If he'd changed his mind... "It's almost time for the alarm clock to go off anyway."

A few minutes later, Sebastian padded into the kitchen and started the coffee. "What's up?" he asked when Wayne joined him.

Instead of grabbing a seat as he normally did, Wayne kept walking until he reached Sebastian. Gripping Sebastian's shoulders, Wayne drew him close enough for a kiss. Their lips met and stayed in contact until Sebastian desperately needed air. He drew back, his lips still tingling from the contact.

"Good morning," Wayne said.

"Morning. I thought—never mind. What did you want to talk about?"

"It's going to take a while for us to work out the logistics of both being with Jen. I don't think she's ready for both of us at the same time yet. We have lots of time. I suggest that whenever the opportunity arises for either of us, we make a move on Jen. Make love to her. Kiss her. Between us we need to woo her around to the idea of both of us."

Sebastian nodded, seeing the sense in Wayne's suggestion. "Do we give each other the opportunity to be alone with Jen?"

"Yeah, I think so. I'm going to be away all weekend. Grandma's ninetieth birthday," Wayne said.

An entire weekend with Jen. Sounded like a plan to him.

When Jen woke the house was silent. She stretched and climbed out of Wayne's big bed. A flush heated her cheeks when she recalled the previous night, the pleasure Wayne had given her without expecting anything in return. Not the norm for most men.

She took the time to remake the bed before leaving the room. A quick shower later, and she walked into the kitchen. Only the lingering scent of toast and the warm coffee pot told of the men's earlier presence.

On the counter, she found a brief note. If she needed help to move more stuff to let them know and they'd help her out after they finished work at six.

"Fine," she muttered. "But how am I meant to get into

town without a car?"

In the end she rang Gaby for a lift to her house.

"So are you with Sebastian and Wayne now?" Gaby asked when Jen climbed into the passenger seat.

Jen shrugged. "Early days."

"I'll bring you those toys later tonight. Will you be at your house or with Wayne and Sebastian?"

"Here," Jen said. "There's a lot to do before settlement date."

"You should definitely have a garage sale."

"Most sales take place at the weekend. There isn't time to organize one."

"The nights are longer with daylight saving. Have a sale tomorrow night. Your house is in the center of town and there's a lot of traffic going past. Ask Ruby at the cafe to put up a sign and pass the word around. I'll tell everyone I see, and you should manage to get a decent crowd."

"It would save packing everything," Jen mused.

"Done deal then. I'm sure I can round up some help for tonight."

Jen gave a decisive nod. "Good idea."

During the next few days Jen scrubbed and cleaned and packed and scrubbed some more. Her helpers arrived at all hours of the day and early evening to give her a hand, the garage sale going even better than she'd imagined. Money for textbooks—sorted.

On Friday morning, she packed the last of her possessions in her car and locked the door on twenty-five years of memories.

Time for a new life.

No one was home when she pulled up into the driveway of her new home. A flicker of disappointment darted through her, pushed aside rapidly by a snort of disgust at herself.

There was no need to rush more than they had already.

About an hour later a car pulled into the driveway. A clatter of boots on the floor, followed by the noiseless steps of a man with a jaunty whistle approached the kitchen.

"Hey, Jen." Wayne snagged her in a gentle but determined manner and drew her close. His lips covered hers before she could even say hello. His brown eyes glowed with mischief when he lifted his head. "Fancy a quickie?"

"Jeez, if that's your best pick-up line it's no wonder you're still single," Sebastian said, appearing behind them.

"Ah, but I'm not single anymore," Wayne said smoothly. "I have both of you to contend with."

"You need two of us to keep you honest," Jen said.

Sebastian barked out a laugh. "Hah! She knows you well."

"Hell, look at the time," Wayne said. "I have to leave in an hour. Come and take a shower with me." He stretched out his hand and smiled at her. "We can have a little nookie."

"I do need a shower." Jen hesitated and glanced at Sebastian in clear doubt. Navigating the waters with one man was bad enough, but two added extra pressure. She'd never thought about that aspect before and didn't know how Gaby managed her two men so adroitly. As she watched, longing crept into Sebastian's face. She started to say no but a quick glance at Wayne changed her mind. Right now she had to choose one of them.

What was the worst that could happen?

She'd have to move out and find new digs. Yeah, like that would be a barrel of fun. Maybe this wasn't such a good idea. "I—"

"Go and shower with Wayne," Sebastian said, retrieving a can of beer from the fridge. "He's going to be away for most of the weekend."

"Yeah, Sebastian will have you all to himself until Sunday evening," Wayne said, putting on a pitiful look.

A laugh exploded from Jen, her unease dissipating. She took his hand and allowed him to tug her down the passage and into the bathroom.

"Let me undress you. I want to see everything I couldn't

see last night."

Rock music with a punchy beat burst to life in the kitchen, distracting her for an instant.

"Don't be shy." Wayne tugged at the scrunchie holding her hair back in a ponytail. Her curls sprang loose and he ran his fingers through the long strands, taking care not to yank her hair. "I can't wait to see you riding my cock, your hair loose and your breasts bouncing up and down."

A tremor sped down her body at the vision he'd pushed into her mind. Wild, uninhibited sex. That wasn't her. Yet last night...

"In the interests of speed why don't we undress ourselves?" Jen whipped her sleeveless shirt over her head and reached behind to unfasten her bra. Her shorts slid over her hips and down her legs with a slight shimmy leaving her dressed only in pale pink panties. A good, lacy pair. Oh yeah. Seemed she was right with the program.

Wayne ripped his gaze off her and started to disrobe. Clothes flew in all directions and seconds later he was naked, his cock at full erection.

Jen switched the water on, grabbed a towel and placed it on the tiled floor. With urgent hands, she angled Wayne under the water and dropped to her knees, using the towel as a pad. "How about I give you something to think about during the weekend?" And grinning up at him, she took his cock into her mouth.

Sebastian listened to the water go on and tried not to think about what the two were doing in there. A burning sensation in his chest hinted at the green-eyed monster trying to claw its way out. He tamped it down in the knowledge that any sort of jealousy would tear them apart before they even started if he let it. Today he'd actually looked forward to coming home. Hell, make that all week. Even though they'd been dog-tired from racing to finish a kitchen and bathroom installation, and he'd been too exhausted to do more than fall into bed at the end of the day, he'd had Wayne at his side. Without even discussing it they'd fallen into sharing a bed, which made Sebastian happy.

There was no reason why he couldn't watch his two favorite people.

Before he'd even finished the thought he found himself halfway down the passage.

He knocked on the door. "Can I watch?"

"Yeah." Wayne's voice emerged low and gritty. Strained.

Not difficult to see why. Jen was on her knees, her mouth full of Wayne's cock. Sebastian stepped nearer while admiring Jen's naked form. She bore healthy curves, and he liked that.

He came to a stop by Jen and placed a hand on her shoulder to let her know he was there. When he glanced down at Wayne's cock all he could see was Jen's hair.

"Want to see?" he asked Wayne. For him, part of the turn-on with oral sex was the visual.

Wayne nodded. "Please."

Sebastian gathered Jen's hair, enjoying the damp softness of the strands running through his fingers. He held the curls away, his gaze caught by the sight of Jen's lips wrapped around Wayne's shaft. "That's so hot." He continued to watch the length of Wayne's dick appear then disappear back into Jen's mouth. The faint sounds she made as she licked and sucked on Wayne pushed at his arousal. He could practically feel the tugs and licks on his own cock. But more than that, the visual gave him ideas.

"Jen, I'm going to come."

Sebastian noticed the faint tremors in Wayne, the grimaces as he tried to keep orgasm at bay. Without thinking too hard, Sebastian knelt awkwardly beside Jen, continuing to hold her hair away from her face with one hand. With his other hand he traced his fingers over Wayne's thigh. "You okay with me touching you?"

"Won't last long," Wayne said through gritted teeth.

"Isn't that the idea? You're on a schedule here." Sebastian tugged on one of Wayne's balls. He tugged firmly then rubbed the smooth skin of Wayne's perineum.

"Holy shit," Wayne muttered, a hard jolt going through him when Sebastian repeated the move.

Beside him Jen made a garbled sound that could have meant anything. Another tremor struck Wayne, and he let out a pained moan. Sebastian watched Jen's throat work in a series of swallows before she pulled away. A droplet of cum glistened on the corner of her mouth. Sebastian leaned closer and licked it off.

Wayne groaned, and both Sebastian and Jen glanced up at him.

"What?" Jen asked.

"That was damn hot. Having both of you at my feet."

Sebastian snorted at Wayne's smug tone.

"Don't you worry, Wayne Garrett," Jen said. "You'll have your turn down on your knees."

Sebastian met Wayne's gaze, heat firing along every single nerve ending in his body. "Would you let me suck you off?"

"In a heartbeat," Wayne said. "Having you touch me like that...you should both experience how that feels. Damn, I wish I didn't have to go away this weekend. I just want time alone with both of you to try everything."

"Everything?" Sebastian asked cautiously. Although he wanted to touch Wayne and kiss him, he didn't know if he was ready for—no! Hell, he'd done anal with a couple of his girlfriends in the past. One of them had loved it and told him exactly what to do, so it wasn't as if he didn't know what the hell he was doing. "You done anal before?"

"No," said Jen.

"Yes," said Wayne at the same time.

"Does it hurt?" Jen asked.

"No idea," Wayne said, and he ducked under the water, pumping a handful of shower gel into his hand at the same time.

"I don't know either," Sebastian said.

They all stared at each other with Wayne's chuckle breaking the silence between them.

"Sounds as if we have some interesting times in store for us," Wayne said, winking at Sebastian.

Sebastian helped Jen to her feet and shunted her under the water with Wayne. He watched Wayne reach out and embrace Jen with one hand. His fingers curled around one of her breasts, his fingers dark against her pale skin. He searched for jealousy within and found nothing this time.

"Do you want a sandwich or something to eat before you go?"

"Do we still have ham?" Wayne turned his gaze on him. It was hot and heady being the recipient of his look and the low level of arousal in Sebastian kicked a notch higher.

Unable to resist, he leaned in and snatched a kiss from Wayne. Hard. Quick. Different.

When Sebastian pulled back he could see the reaction in Wayne, the swift flare of need, and it warmed him. "Later," he mouthed, and with a wink at Jen he went to make a couple of sandwiches.

Lucky he'd followed his impulse to go to the bathroom and watch. Anticipation simmered through him, part of him impatient for the weeks to come. Still, he had this weekend and nothing but free time to explore all sorts of things with Jen.

Good times.

Chapter Seven

WAYNE LEFT AFTER KISSING them both. Jen didn't feel dirty or sluttish or even selfish for taking two men off the market. Instead she felt lucky. Happy.

She cuddled into Sebastian's side and waved as Wayne drove off.

"What would you like to do? Fancy a couple of drinks at The Thirsty Cricket? I saw Liam earlier today, and he said they were heading to the pub for dinner. There's a live band tonight."

"Sounds good. I might even corner Gaby and ask nosy questions. She'll know if it hurts."

"I suppose I could ask Liam," Sebastian said, but his tone was doubtful.

Jen pictured the possible scenarios and the way that conversation could go. "Maybe you should let me do the asking."

"Yeah, but it's probably different for guys."

"Go shower," Jen said. "We might as well have dinner there too." She turned away, then said over her shoulder, "You might even be able to persuade me to wear my vibrator. I don't mind you having the control." A grin formed at his groan, and she made sure she twitched her butt until she'd disappeared from his sight.

THEY ENDED UP SHARING a large table with Gaby and her men. The pub was packed, the doors and windows thrown open and some of the crowd spilling out to the beer garden at the back.

"Let's dance," Sebastian said.

Jen whispered, "Do you have the control I gave you?"

Sebastian groaned, grabbed her hand and towed her over to the small dance floor. He pulled her against his body, making no secret of the fact they were together romantically. Jen caught the curious glances sent their direction by some locals and a couple of the women looked distinctly envious.

Too bad. *Her man now.*

She swayed in time to the music but they didn't move around the floor. It was too crowded for that. One song blurred into another, only the sudden vibration in her pussy jolting her from her dreamy state.

She gripped Sebastian's shoulders and grinned up at him. "I thought you'd forgotten."

"Not a chance," he drawled. "I intend to keep you on edge until you're desperate. Then we'll go home."

"Sounds good to me. Win-win all the way around." *Oh-oh.* Sebastian's ex-wife had come in with a group of girlfriends. Damn. She wasn't sure if she should say something or not. "Sebastian, your ex is here."

"Don't care," he said. "As long as I don't have to talk to her everything will work out fine."

"You don't miss her?"

"We're divorced. I'm well rid of her."

Victoria, his ex, was attractive with an air of sexy about her. No one would mistake her for the girl next door. Jen watched her, saw the moment she realized Sebastian was present and the way she narrowed her eyes. Jen decided she didn't want to talk to the ex either, not that they ran in the same circles.

An insistent buzz from the vibrator focused her attention exactly where Sebastian wanted it. On him. She blew him a kiss and the vibrations trailed off. "When we get back to the house, where would you like me to touch you first? What would you like me to do to you?"

"I get a choice?" His eyes darkened with unexpected mischief, and her heart twisted with joy. Sebastian didn't smile much, and it was good to see him in this mood.

"You get to think about it for the entire night until we get home, and you're not rushing me off because I intend to discuss a few things with Gaby first."

"Why don't you call her and go out to lunch tomorrow? Have a girls' outing."

"You wouldn't mind me doing that?"

"Of course not. I have a couple of things I need to take care of at the job site tomorrow morning anyway. Jen, I already know what I want to do the minute we get home."

"Oh?" Her brows rose in a silent invitation for him to share.

"Yeah. I want you to undress me, one item of clothing at a time. A few touches and kisses would be good, then I want to strip off your clothes, toss you on the bed and slide my cock inside you until I'm balls-deep. I want to feel your heat and your pussy clutching my cock."

Each husky word tugged at her breasts and echoed in her womb. Her body softened and moistened. The vibrations started again—an easy buzz that sent her toward the edge but not enough to throw her into orgasm.

Jen cleared her throat and worked on holding back vocal sounds of pleasure. "Is that all?"

"I'll kiss you and play with your breasts until I know exactly what you like best. And all the time I'll be stroking into you deep and steady, driving us until we both explode." He paused, his pale eyes gleaming. "Is that the sort of thing you had in mind?"

The vibrations picked up in speed, and she bit her bottom lip to stem her moan of desperation. "Yeah," she whispered. "You do good sex talk. Uh, should I tell you what I want to do to you?"

"Do you think you'll have the energy once I'm finished?" His tone held smugness and a hint of challenge.

"I haven't had a chance to look through the stuff Gaby gave me to test. I'm sure there's something in there to help pierce your attitude."

The vibrator speed kicked up, and with it, Sebastian's smirk. "You shouldn't try to challenge me when I have the remote."

Suddenly, it was too much for her. A moan burst from her and she clutched Sebastian's wide shoulders as the spasms weakened her knees. Sebastian's soft chuckle brought swift color to her cheeks, and she ducked her head. A tug of fear pierced her, stirring in the pit of her stomach. Had anyone noticed? God, she'd die of embarrassment if the dancers around them had witnessed her...ah...obvious enjoyment.

"It's okay," Sebastian whispered.

It was difficult to miss the humor in his tone or the vibrations against her cheek. A swift glance up at his face confirmed her suspicions. The louse was laughing. A flash of chagrin struck and she started talking, standing on tiptoe to speak against his ear. "You and Wayne will want to fuck each other eventually."

A jolt went through Sebastian, his muscles tensing beneath her hands. She had his full attention. Now it was time to reel him in.

"I'm sure Gaby has some anal toys in her bag of tricks," Jen continued. "And I know for a fact that some of them vibrate. Imagine this. Me undressing you slowly, kissing and biting every inch of skin I uncover. Waking up your nerve endings until you're one big bundle of anticipation." She paused to imagine the scenario. A wicked grin reshaped her mouth. She'd see exactly how he handled walking off the dance floor with a giant hard-on. "Then, I'd go to work on your jeans."

His husky groan prompted a wider grin. She'd teach him to tease her in a public place.

"You're wearing tight jeans that cling to every inch of your sexy butt. Your cock is a hard bulge. I glide my fingers over it and on the next pass I use my fingernails. They make a scratchy sound against the denim. I struggle with the button on your fly and you get all impatient. You tear my fumbling fingers away before I can protest and you try to wrench it down." Jen dug her fingernails into his biceps to make sure he was paying attention. Satisfied by his husky groan, she continued, "I smack your hands away and slide down the zipper. The rasp is loud..."

"Go on," he said in a tight voice.

"Don't you think we should go back to the table?"

"Why—?" He broke off when he noticed the dance floor was emptying, and they were receiving funny looks. "Shit." Grabbing her hand, he towed her back to their spot.

She couldn't help it. She let her gaze flicker to his groin and took great satisfaction in seeing the distinct ridge of his erection. They slid onto their seats, joining Gaby and Fletch. Liam was nowhere to be seen.

"Do we need another drink or should I continue?" Jen asked.

"Drink," Sebastian muttered, already jumping to his feet. "You guys ready for another one?"

"Thanks," Fletch said.

"Coward."

Sebastian scowled at her, but she didn't hold back on her grin. Jen watched him disappear into the crowd.

"What did you do to him?" Gaby asked.

"Payback is a bitch, and if he thinks I've exacted enough

punishment yet, he should think again."

"Should I ask you what he did?" Fletch asked.

"Gaby's fault," Jen said with a stern glance at her friend.

"Me? I didn't do anything."

"Her sex toys?" Fletch guessed.

"Sebastian is learning that teasing goes both ways, and I'm not willing to sit back like a good submissive. I want full participation."

"Go, Jen!" Gaby lifted her hand for a high five, and Jen smacked her palm against her friend's.

"I wonder if I should warn him," Fletch mused.

"I'm sure he's intelligent enough to figure it out on his own," Jen said sweetly. She turned back to Gaby. "Are you doing anything tomorrow? I want to ask you a few questions, and Sebastian suggested we do lunch."

Amusement highlighted a dimple at the corner of Fletch's mouth. "Not in those words, I bet."

"Of course not. There's nothing girly about Sebastian." True. He was all smoldering man and, like an iceberg, most of his personality remained hidden until he chose to share himself. Acute anticipation simmered at a low-level burn, tugging at her sex. She squeezed her thighs together and held her breath as she rode out the tiny quivers that rocked her.

"Jen?"

Eyes that she hadn't remembered closing flew open in consternation. Good grief. She needed privacy and a naked Sebastian. In that order. She determinedly ignored the blood rushing to her cheeks. "Sorry. Just spaced out for a moment there."

"I thought you weren't intending to wear that vibrator with the remote control again."

"Sebastian is very persuasive when he sets his mind to it, but no, it wasn't the vibrator. Lunch? Can you meet me tomorrow?"

"Why don't you drop by my place and we'll have lunch and a few drinks there. Sebastian can pick you up, so you won't need to worry about driving."

Jen nodded. "Sounds good. I'll make a quiche and bring it for lunch."

"Excellent plan," Gaby said. "I'll make a couple of salads. You should try this with Sebastian." She leaned close and whispered in Gaby's ear.

"Really?"

"Oh yeah. He'll like it. Just use—"

"Plenty of lube," Jen finished for her friend. She nodded. "I can do that."

Fletch's brows drew together. "Should I ask?"

"I'll demonstrate later tonight," Gaby promised.

"Will I like it?"

"Your eyes will cross in a good way."

Fletch's eyebrows drew together, and Jen could see his mind turning with the possibilities. "Maybe we'll leave soon."

Sebastian arrived back with drinks. After distributing them, he sat beside Jen and slipped his arm around her. It was natural, done without thought on his part, and the action warmed her all the way through. She leaned in to him, and after a quick wink at Gaby, continued with her seduction by whispering in his ear.

"Instead of the black cotton underwear I expect, your cock springs out, hot and hard beneath my fingers."

Sebastian's arm tightened around her shoulders, yet his expression didn't change. She needed to mess with him some more.

"I scoop out your cock and run my finger along the length of your shaft. My fingers run over the head and under, teasing you where you're most sensitive. I add my mouth, dragging my tongue across the flared head. I pause to taste a drop of pre-cum. It's tart, a little salty. You're moving your hips in tiny jerks, pushing your cock deeper into my mouth. I pull on your cock with some suction, and you moan, your hands digging into my hair. It hurts, but it's a good pain. I hum my appreciation, the vibrations dragging a groan from you. You sound as if you're in pain, but I know better. You've started to tremble. Pre-cum is seeping from your slit in a constant stream, and I have to lick a lot to keep up. I take you deeper and let one of my hands roam over your balls. They're hard and I know you're not far away from orgasm. I reach between your legs and glide my fingers over your pucker—"

Sebastian sprang to his feet and grabbed her hand. "We're going home." He dragged her two steps before she could protest.

"Wait! I haven't finished...my drink."

"You can have a *drink* at home." His emphasis told her he knew exactly which corner her mind had turned.

"See you tomorrow," Gaby called, laughter in her voice. "Come around eleven."

The drive home seemed to take ages even though Sebastian drove much faster than usual. They pulled up in the driveway, and Jen removed her seatbelt.

"Wait there."

Sebastian climbed out and rounded the vehicle to open her door. He helped her out and grabbed her hand, lacing their fingers together. Jen's pulse rate clicked up a few notches. The touch seemed intimate yet felt so right.

"I hope you're not tired."

"Nope," she said cheerfully.

"Wayne's room?"

"Yes." Although Wayne wasn't here she liked the thought of spending time with Sebastian in Wayne's bed. "I wish he was here with us."

"Me too, but I think we can manage to entertain ourselves."

Jen thought of Gaby's suggestion and fought to contain her smile. "I think you're right."

Without warning, Sebastian swept her into his arms and in seconds flat they were in Wayne's bedroom. Jen struggled a fraction to let Sebastian know she wanted down. He dropped her on the mattress and switched on one of the bedside lamps. Despite Wayne's absence, she could smell the citrus of his favored aftershave. He'd left a pair of jeans over the back of a chair and obviously emptied his pockets of change before leaving. A handful of coins littered the top of a set of wooden drawers.

Sebastian straightened to glower down at her, his feet planted hip width apart. "Take off your clothes."

Jen scrambled off the bed. "It's still my turn. Stay there and don't move a muscle until I tell you."

Sebastian looked as if he might argue. Finally, he gave a curt nod, his gaze tracking her as she ambled toward him. With nimble fingers, she unbuttoned his shirt, leaning forward to nibble at the swell of one pectoral muscle. He drew in a sharp breath but didn't move. Gradually, she divested him of his shirt and knelt in front of him to remove his boots and socks.

"Now the good part," she said.

"Next time." He exploded into a flurry of movement. He undressed her in seconds flat, tossing her clothes over the floor. His remaining clothes disappeared just as quickly. "Better."

Jen stared at him, unable to glance away even if she'd wanted to. His grin stole her breath, made her desperate to touch and kiss him, show him some affection. Part of her wondered how she'd come to be in this position—naked with Sebastian. It was enough to make a girl giddy.

"You do want this?" His scrutiny pierced her, flaying her wide open, and she suspected he saw more than she was comfortable with.

She laughed lightly to shift her unease. "On the bed. I'll show you exactly how much I want to be with you." When he didn't move fast enough for her liking, Jen pounced, pushing him down on the mattress. His light blue eyes widened, a slow grin tugging at his lips again.

Jen didn't give him a chance to regroup. She straddled his hips, letting her hands wander over his beautiful body. Muscles sculpted by hard, physical work. Warm skin. And an erection, strong and thick with a ruddy head. "You're very tempting."

"Fair warning. If you don't hurry this along, I'm going to take control."

A chuckle burst from her. "Don't you believe in foreplay?"

"When I'm the one doing the playing," he muttered.

"Hands-on kinda guy, huh?"

"Believe it." Once again he exploded into action, using his strength to overpower her. A squeak escaped her, although he didn't hurt her. She found herself caged between his arms and the mattress, staring up into his handsome face. His lips descended, and she didn't consider fighting for freedom because it didn't matter either way. She was right where she wanted to be.

Her arms curled around his neck, holding him close. His scent washed over her, again the hint of citrus with an underlying masculine scent that made her think of the wild outdoors and windswept beaches. His erection slid over the smooth skin of her stomach, leaving a wet trail. Her pussy pulsed in recognition. "Condom?"

"Thank god," Sebastian said in a fervent voice. He reached for a bedside drawer and pulled out a handful of condoms. "Want to try some of the lube?"

Jen grinned. "You can never have enough lube."

"Someone listens to Gaby's lectures."

"Yeah. Hard not to absorb some of what she says."

Sebastian parted her legs, baring her to his gaze. He slipped a finger inside her and removed the remote vibrator. It left her feeling empty. She squirmed a little, trying to find something to rub against, something to soothe the ache riding her.

"Steady." With the condom in place, Sebastian opened the bottle of lube and squeezed some onto his hand. The cool sensation did nothing to bank down her need. Instead it ramped it up, the icy chill morphing to fiery heat.

She gasped. "Sebastian. Now. No more mucking around. Please."

Without another word, he positioned himself and pushed deep.

"Yes," she said with a hiss of pleasure. Her fingers dug into his backside, silently encouraging him to go faster, harder. The next stroke almost made her eyes cross, the pleasure sizzling across her skin, growing bigger, hotter. "Sebastian, please."

"What do you need?"

"Touch me."

His finger slid between them, rubbing across her clit.

"Yes! Just there." A familiar shimmer started. The sensation streaked down her legs, then the pulses began. Hard spasms that seemed to go on forever. She sighed and clutched Sebastian's shoulders more tightly. She gasped when his strong drive into her elicited another robust pulse.

"Damn, that feels good. I like the way you grip my cock. I want this to last."

Gaby's advice chose that moment to flash into prominence. "Where's the lube?"

"Why do you want it?"

"Me to know," she whispered in a seductive voice. She spied the bottle and grabbed it, thumbing the lid open. "Carry on," she said when he paused in his thrusts. "Don't worry about holding on. We can do this again." She spoke against his ear. "We have all night." Her tongue lashed his earlobe before delving delicately inside. While he was distracted, she caressed one butt cheek. The fingers of her other hand stroked across his pucker. He froze.

"What are you doing?"

"Just trying something Gaby suggested."

"You discuss us with Gaby?" Now he sounded pissed.

"Don't be silly. Any discussion is only in generalities. I'd never give away any secrets about either you or Wayne. Besides, I told you I intended to ask questions."

Sebastian cleared his throat. "Shit, I wasn't thinking. Of course you wouldn't."

Instead of commenting further, she ran her finger back and forth. Some of the tension left Sebastian until she pushed her finger into him. He froze again.

"Don't tense up. I just want to make you feel good."

"You haven't got anything up your arse."

"Jeez, it's just a fingertip. You probably figure you'll fuck my arse at some stage. Makes sense since there are two of you. You and Wayne have kissed. You intend to do more. Right?"

"Maybe."

"Then don't be such a baby." She pushed her finger deeper and slid it back out. When he didn't protest she repeated the move, massaging inside him. He thrust into her again, his cock harder and larger than before. His strokes became erratic, his breaths noisy. She could feel his racing pulse and gloried in the knowledge she was doing that to him. She held his pleasure in her hands, and being with Sebastian, with Wayne, it felt so right. Perfect. She moved her finger around, searching. His body twitched without warning. He groaned. Ah, there. She'd found the right spot.

"Jen." He shuddered when she moved her finger back and forth. His hips jerked, and he did two rapid strokes before freezing in place. He stayed right where he was until Jen removed her finger.

"You're heavy."

"Sorry." Another groan slipped from him as he lifted off

her and dealt with the condom. "Damn, the bloody thing broke."

"You'd better make a note of the batch number for Gaby. She'll want to know."

"The condom broke," Sebastian repeated.

Jen yawned. "No problem. I'm on the Pill."

"Oh. Good," he said finally. "Come and have a shower with me." He waggled his butt and looked over his shoulder to wink at her. "We have one of those waterproof duck things."

"Another of Gaby's vibrators?"

"Yeah. You interested?"

"You and Wayne are full of surprises," she said, taking his hand. Somehow it didn't seem to matter that they were naked.

"Stick around, Jen. You ain't seen nothing yet."

Chapter Eight

IT WAS SILLY TO be nervous about going to school.
Sebastian had kept her mind off her first day by keeping
her busy for all of Saturday. Now it was Sunday and school
loomed like UFOs on the Sloan horizon.

Sebastian buzzed a kiss across her cheek. "What's up?"

"I'm apprehensive about school tomorrow. All the kids
are so much younger."

"You'll be fine." Sebastian handed her a cup of coffee.
"All you need to do is keep your head down and hand in
your assignments. You don't need to worry about boy-girl
stuff because—newsflash—you're taken."

"You make it sound easy." She remembered her school
days, even if she had left early to look after her mother. "All
the cliques. Navigating them is hard. Scary."

"Don't forget the kids in your class are new to this too."

"But they know each other."

"Honestly, Jen. You get on well with everyone. You won't have any problems."

Easy for him to say. "It's closer to lunch time than breakfast. Should I make a bacon and egg pie?"

"Wayne has a sweet tooth. Why don't we make some cookies too?"

"Anything to keep my mind off tomorrow."

It was fun working with Sebastian in the kitchen. Between snatched kisses and lingering touches, they managed to make the pie and two batches of chocolate chip cookies. They ate outside on the deck and talked about her school courses and Sebastian's and Wayne's plans for their business. And they discussed Wayne.

"Do you think Wayne is serious about both of us?" Sebastian asked.

"I think so, but anything could happen." Jen hesitated before deciding to go with honesty. "Things might not go as smoothly once people in the town learn we're not sharing a house for convenience. You and I don't have any close family left, but Wayne does even if they don't actually live in the town."

Some of the happiness seeped out of Sebastian, and she wished she'd kept her doubts to herself.

"Do you think Wayne's family will put pressure on him?"

"Sebastian, once I finish school, I'm going to leave Sloan and go to university. It's what I've always wanted." She needed to keep things real.

"Yeah, I know. I admire you for going after what you want. Would you like to go for a walk?" Sebastian asked in a rapid change of subject.

"Sure." Jen stood and took his outstretched hand.

Together they ambled from the deck, taking a path leading down to the Sloan River. The track ran through a stand of native trees, and the leaf litter crunched beneath their sandals. It was cool under the canopy, a fresh green scent tickling her nose. A respite from the summer sun.

Maybe moving in with Wayne and Sebastian wasn't such a good idea. If she were wise she'd tell them she'd move out. She thought about that and rejected the idea immediately, because the last two days spent with Sebastian had been so much fun. The sex was incredible, and the little time she'd spent fooling around with Wayne rated as special too. They'd been friends of sort ever since she'd worked for them—well, acquaintances—and since her leaving party their familiarity had changed for the better. No, she didn't want to walk away. *But she'd walk away the minute she finished at school...*

"Want to have a swim?"

Jen's gaze fastened on Sebastian. "Skinny dipping? What

if someone decides to walk down the river path?" Despite her protest, even she caught the note of intrigue hovering in her voice.

"We'll hear them coming," Sebastian said. "Besides, all we need to do is keep under the water. They won't suspect a thing."

"You don't think the piles of clothes on the riverbank might give them a clue?" Yet the idea of a swim appealed to her. "I suppose we could hide until they walk past."

Sebastian chuckled, his hand tightening on hers. She was becoming addicted to his rare smiles and couldn't help grinning back at him. In this mood he was irresistible.

"Yes! We could do that. I—" His cell phone started to ring. He glanced at the screen. "It's Wayne." He flipped open his phone. "We're down by the river. Yep. We're going to have a swim. You coming down? Okay. See you in ten." He ended the call and shoved the cell phone back in his pocket. "He's arrived home early and is coming to swim with us."

"You know you can't do anything too kinky out here in the open, right?"

Sebastian waggled his brows. "The bits under the water won't show. Last one in the water is a rotten egg." Sebastian was half naked before he realized she wasn't moving. "What's wrong?"

"I like watching you."

"You'd better hurry before I pick you up and dump you in the water, clothes and all."

She backed up two steps. "You wouldn't!"

"Try me." He kicked off his sandals and peeled off his shorts and underwear. Naked, he prowled closer.

"Bully."

"Or I might just jump you instead." His eyes gleamed as he took another step toward her.

"I can hear someone coming."

"It's probably Wayne."

"Not unless he's wearing a bright pink T-shirt."

Sebastian glanced in the direction she indicated, let out a ripe curse and scuttled toward the river. He kicked a stone, swore again and practically fell into the water. Jen saw a flash of white bottom, and a giggle burst from her.

"Is it cold?"

"I stubbed my toe," Sebastian said.

Still grinning, Jen started to collect Sebastian's clothes together.

"Jen, what are you doing here?" Richard Morgan, one of the Fancy Free board members, and his wife Hinekiri came to a halt in front of her.

An arm slid around her shoulders, and she jumped, letting out a small *eek* of alarm.

"Steady."

Some of the adrenaline settled when she recognized the low voice, whispering in her ear.

"We're about to go skinny dipping," Wayne said smoothly.

Jen wasn't sure where to look.

"Those sorts of shenanigans can get a girl in trouble," Hinekiri said.

"And you would be talking from experience," Richard said in a gruff voice.

Hinekiri's unusual violet eyes twinkled with mischief. "Of course. Come, Richard. Let's leave the youngsters to their naughtiness." She waggled her fingers in a gesture of goodbye. "Have fun. And tell Sebastian he needs to find a fast-flowing piece of water if he expects to hide his nudity."

"Hinekiri!" Richard said gruffly, although his eyes glittered with amusement.

"I can't help it if I have good eyesight."

"But you don't have to look. See you later," Richard said, hustling his wife down the river path.

Jen grinned after the retreating couple. Gaby said the board meetings at Fancy Free were a lot of fun, and Jen could well believe it. The board members were elderly, but they weren't slow of mind.

"Did you miss me?" Wayne ripped his gaze off the faint mark on Jen's neck and focused on her mouth instead. His grandmother's birthday party had come at a bad time. He'd thought about Sebastian and Jen the entire weekend, about what they might be doing. Together. He held his arms out in silent invitation, hoping like hell he wasn't making a giant mistake. Being away from Sloan had given him too much damn time to think.

But Jen didn't hesitate. She threw herself at him, and he wrapped his arms around her, some of his angst fading away. Their lips met and instantly, Wayne felt better with the intimate contact. He kissed her lazily, keeping things casual rather than frightening her with the intensity of feelings coursing through him. Her obvious enjoyment pushed away the remnants of his anxiety. They were still okay. He'd let his imagination run away with him.

"Hey! Are you two coming in or not?"

Wayne's arms tensed before he eased up on the embrace. No jealousy. This was his best friend. Sebastian would rather rip off his right arm than hurt him. *But you haven't wanted the same girl before*. And he hadn't kissed and touched his best friend intimately before either.

"Did you have a good time at the party?" Jen kicked off her sandals and started to undress.

"Sure." If he didn't think too hard about all the "When

135

are you going to settle down?" questions. Shoving aside the fruitless thoughts in his head, he stripped off his clothes.

He followed Jen down to the water, taking the time to admire her curvy form. She headed straight to Sebastian, leaping at him and creating a huge splash. Sebastian laughed, the sound light and carefree. Something in Wayne knotted, pulling so tight he struggled to draw breath. They were comfortable together. At ease.

Wayne entered the water, some of his earlier relief fading as he waded closer to the couple.

"Wayne," Sebastian said. "How is your grandmother? Did she have a good time?"

Wayne dredged up strength he hadn't known he'd possessed. A smile curved his stiff lips. "We managed to surprise her."

"We missed you." Sebastian released Jen and grabbed Wayne. "I want a kiss too."

Wayne's mouth dropped open in surprise, and Sebastian took advantage. His tongue slid inside, and he curled a hand around Wayne's head drawing him closer, taking the kiss into lover territory. A soft body pressed into him from behind, surrounding him in warmth and strength. A hard cock dug into his hip bone while stiff nipples stabbed his back.

"I need you around to help keep Sebastian in line," Jen whispered.

The tension drained from him. *Stupid.* He'd let his mind get the better of him. All the well-meaning questions from his family had propelled him into jealousy.

"We've been experimenting with Gaby's sex toys," Jen said.

The wall he'd managed to re-erect in his mind started to tear apart.

"We decided we're going to practice everything we've learned on you," Sebastian said. "I hope you're not too tired after the drive back from Taupo."

"Should I be worried?"

"Only if you're frightened of too much pleasure." Jen's hand slipped between him and Sebastian and closed around Wayne's shaft. "We can start now." She nuzzled his neck. "Give you a taste of what we mean."

"Let me jerk him off," Sebastian said. "You can take care of the other stuff."

"What other stuff?"

Sebastian's callused hand replaced Jen's softer one.

"What other stuff?" Wayne repeated.

"Nothing bad," Sebastian whispered, seconds before he claimed Wayne's mouth and put a halt to further conversation.

The cool river water didn't put a dent in the heat that rocketed through him. A hard mouth kissed him while Sebastian never let up on the hand action. Confident strokes propelled him toward climax, aided by the fact he hadn't had sex in any shape or form since he'd left home.

His eyes drifted closed and every sense intensified. The rush of the water over the stones added a musical accompaniment as did the song of a nearby thrush. The sun shone down on their naked shoulders, a direct contrast to the temperature of the water. Every inch of his skin tingled, sensitive to the touch of Sebastian and Jen's hands. While Sebastian kissed him and continued with the excellent hand action, Jen stroked his balls, tugged them and ran her fingers all over his backside. He started when she ran a finger from his balls up to his arsehole.

"Steady," she whispered in his ear. "We just want to make you feel good."

Hell. They were sure shooting holes in his jealousy. He couldn't think, couldn't put his stray thoughts together when they were touching him like this. The firm tugging on his balls made him realize how quickly they'd propelled him toward climax. He was only a hairsbreadth away from tumbling into white-hot pleasure. Then Jen rubbed his pucker, pushing insistently. Sebastian pulled on his cock. Wayne felt the intrusion of Jen's finger, foreign but not painful. Excitement burst through him. He moaned against Sebastian's lips and came, his entire body twitching, caught in a violent maelstrom, his mind blank of everything except the sexual satisfaction.

When he came back to himself, he realized that Jen and Sebastian were the only things holding him afloat. He struggled to find his footing, his body strangely lethargic after his orgasm.

"Think what we could have done if we'd—"

"Had lube!" Sebastian finished Jen's sentence.

"You two are entirely too pleased with yourselves."

Sebastian grinned. "If you want to mutter about payback I'm up for that. Anytime."

"I'm happy to sign up for payback too," Jen chirped.

Wayne sent them a disgruntled glare. "Don't think the pair of you can gang up on me."

"Why not?" Jen asked.

"It's working so far," Sebastian added.

Wayne burst into action without warning. He dunked Sebastian under the water and turned to Jen. "Your turn."

She let out a girly screech and splashed him with water before ducking under the surface and disappearing from sight.

Half an hour later, exhausted from their play, they waded out of the river and took possession of a sunny spot on a grassy bank.

"I'm feeling incredibly horny," Jen said. "I wish we'd thought to bring condoms with us."

Her words surprised a laugh from him. "Is this our shy office assistant talking?"

"You forget. I'm a student now."

"We can fix your problem without condoms, Jen." Sebastian arched his brows. "Want to have some fun?"

"Which end do you want?"

Sebastian shook his head. "Both. Why don't we work in tandem? That way we can kiss each other at the same time."

"What do you want me to do?" Jen asked. "And isn't this a little too public for anything like that? It's bad enough that I'm sitting here butt-naked."

"We'll hear anyone coming. I promise," Wayne said.

"Yeah, as long as you don't make too much noise," Sebastian said. "Top end first."

Wayne followed Sebastian's directives. His friend seemed a changed man from the one he'd left on Friday night. He'd lost his brittle edge, looking more like a content jungle cat.

"Kiss me?" Sebastian stared at him with open yearning.

It was the same way he looked at Jen, a wealth of need in his pale blue eyes. Pretty eyes, Wayne realized. Long dark lashes surrounded eyes that were currently stormy with passion. Wayne curled a hand around the back of Sebastian's neck. "Jen, lie flat on your back and part your legs enough to feel the breeze on your pussy. Watch me kiss Sebastian." Wayne settled into the kiss straightaway with no seductive preliminaries. Instantly a spear of lust struck him and tension increased in his groin as blood lengthened his shaft.

"I don't think I'll ever get tired of watching the two of you together," Jen whispered. "I didn't realize it would be such a turn on to watch. We should take a movie of us together. I think I'd like that."

Wayne pulled back, and Sebastian groaned a protest. "Do you like people watching you?"

"Me?" Sebastian asked.

"Question works for both of you."

"I've never thought about it," Sebastian said.

Jen's brow puckered. "Giles wanted to film us together, and I wouldn't let him."

A growl emerged from Sebastian, and the same protest rumbled in Wayne's chest. Hell no!

"He would've put it on the web," Wayne said, certainty twisting his gut. "Are you sure he didn't tape you?"

Sebastian frowned. "I wouldn't put it past him to do something sneaky."

Jen's smile died. "I'm sure he didn't film us. Besides, his pasty white butt would be in the movie too."

Wayne glanced at Sebastian, and his friend gave a curt nod in return. They'd check it out the next time they saw Giles.

"Your turn, Jen. Are you ready?" Sebastian asked.

She snorted. "I told you I was horny."

Wayne let out a *tsking* sound. "We can't have that." He bent over to kiss her cheek before aiming a kiss at the corner of her mouth.

Sebastian mirrored his actions, letting his mouth linger and blend into a three-way kiss at times.

"Keep your legs parted," Wayne said. "We want to be able to see if we're doing a good job." He went back to kissing her mouth, one of his hands tracing a path around the curve of her breast. Sebastian followed his lead without hesitation, and Wayne let himself drift into pleasure. His cock was hard, but he didn't worry about getting himself off. This was for Jen. He trailed kisses down the column of her neck, breathing in the faint scent of the soap. A sense of rightness filled him when he realized that Sebastian's body held a trace of the same lemony smell.

Wayne lifted his head and reached for Sebastian. The abrasion of stubble no longer took him by surprise. Instead he concentrated on the rub of lips, the slide of tongues and the tug of desire. The more he kissed and touched Sebastian, the more he realized how comfortable the exchange of intimacies felt. Natural. When he let his mind drift to sex with Sebastian, that's when he hit a brick wall.

"Wayne? Is someone coming?" The urgency in Jen's voice made him chuckle.

"No one is coming. No one except you," he promised. He tugged on her thigh and she reluctantly unclenched them, parting her legs again.

Sebastian licked around a nipple.

"You like that," Wayne said. "Your nipples have turned hard again, like they were when we walked out of the water."

A breathless groan sounded, and Wayne saw that Sebastian was drawing on the tip, his cheeks hollowing with the suction. He hurriedly followed suit to give Jen a twin sensation.

They played and teased her, nibbling on her flesh, licking and driving her arousal higher. Gradually, they moved down her body. A nip at her hip. The dip of tongues into her navel, the lick along the top of her thigh.

Wayne lifted his head. "Your legs need to be a little wider. That's it. Look how wet she is."

"We're going to lick that sweet moisture away,"

Sebastian whispered.

A shudder went through Wayne. When he glanced down at his cock he saw a pearl of pre-cum beading in his slit. Hell. He'd give almost anything to have their mouths on his cock right now. Both of them. He glanced at Sebastian's cock and noticed he was in an even worse state. "You're next," Wayne whispered, realizing something else. Even more than having their mouths on him, he wanted to give Sebastian the same experience. There were three of them, and there was no room for selfish actions. No room for jealousy either.

"Her clit is swollen. I bet it won't take much for her to go off," Wayne said.

"Enough talk," Jen protested. "Do something!"

After a quick glance at Sebastian, Wayne lowered his head. He licked along the outer rim of one plump fold. His tongue went lower to her entrance and licked away some of her juices. Sebastian's tongue battled with his and sparks shot down Wayne's spine. His balls lifted, the soft breeze across the sensitive head of his cock almost too much to bear. Wayne sucked in a deep breath.

Concentrate on Jen.

He licked his way to her clit, and lightly rubbed the nub with the tip of his tongue. Sebastian's tongue tangled with his and together they teased Jen's clit. Her hips lifted, pushing into their touch. She groaned. Their tongues danced around and over her clit again and Jen came apart, shuddering and groaning as she shattered.

A foreign sound pierced Wayne's consciousness. Fuck! Someone was coming. He jumped up and grabbed the piles of clothes, flinging them at Jen and Sebastian. "Get dressed. Someone is heading this way."

Wayne pulled on his shorts and yanked a blue T-shirt over his head. Seconds later, Richard and Hinekiri appeared on the path.

"See. I told you we wouldn't be interrupting anything," Hinekiri said with a toothy grin.

"That would be why Wayne is wearing a T-shirt too small for him and Jen's shirt is too big." Richard's voice held wry humor.

Hinekiri chortled. "Oh, and Sebastian has his shorts on inside out."

"You shouldn't be looking at Sebastian's shorts," Jen muttered.

"On that we agree," Richard said. "Let's go."

Hinekiri winked at Wayne. "But I wanted to ask nosy questions."

"I think we've embarrassed Jen enough," Richard said firmly, guiding his wife along the path. "They're just lucky we're not tied up with the Sloan Gazette and Ms.

Knowall."

"Ms. Knowall!" Jen looked a little sick, and Wayne felt distinct sympathy. He didn't want their relationship emblazoned all over the local gossip column either. "We'll finish this at home," he said.

Sebastian's eyes gleamed. "Plenty of lube and condoms there."

Chapter Nine

Wayne had seemed a bit off when he'd first arrived. If Sebastian didn't know better he'd suspect jealousy. As they walked single file down the track, heading back to the house, Sebastian turned the idea around in his mind. Jealousy? Nah, it couldn't be. Wayne was one of the most easy-going guys he knew. He didn't sulk or pout or often lose his temper. He was an open book.

"I sorted out the few problems we had onsite," Sebastian said. "I think we'll finish ahead of time after all."

"Good. That's good. So what did you guys do while I was away?"

The idea of envy and maybe a little resentment slid right back into Sebastian's mind. Wayne wasn't acting like his usual confident self. Did he want Sebastian to back off or did he need time alone with Jen?

"We went to the Cricket for dinner and met up with

Gaby, Fletch and Liam. Did a little dancing..." Jen trailed off, and Sebastian wished he could see her face. He enjoyed seeing the slow wash of color travel up her neck until it stained her cheeks.

"We fucked like bunnies," Sebastian said. No need for secrets. If they started keeping things from each other then mistrust would bloom.

Up ahead, Wayne stopped walking, almost causing a pileup. He turned to face Sebastian. "Was it good? Did you even think of me?"

Whoa! The big green-eyed monster.

Jen reached out, placed her hand on Wayne's tense shoulder. "Of course we missed you. We're a team. Isn't that what we decided?"

Sebastian heard some of the confidence leach out of her toward the end of her speech. "We thought about you. We talked about you. And when we get back to the house we're going to jump you to show you exactly how much we missed you."

Jen nodded. "What he said."

Sebastian liked the return of her self-assurance and also the pleased expression on Wayne's face.

"Sorry." A chagrined smile changed the set of his mouth for an instant before it faded. "I spent all weekend dodging the single women my grandmother had invited to meet me and hearing from my aunties and mother how it was past time for me to settle down with a family. Messed with my head."

Having seen Wayne's adopted family in action before Sebastian could understand some of the stress in his friend. It was early days yet, and this *thing* between them required work and finesse. But they had time to work out the dynamics and explore the possibilities. He knew what he wanted from Wayne and Jen. A family. But he'd had longer to think about the possibilities. They needed time too.

Wayne continued down the track, and he and Jen fell into line. Once they reached the house, Sebastian started to issue orders.

"Keep going to your bedroom. By the time I arrive I want to see you both naked."

Wayne cocked his head. "What are you going to do?"

"I'm going to lock the door, on the off-chance we have visitors, and I'll grab a few things from the stuff Gaby gave to Jen. The box is still in your room, right?"

"Yeah. Make sure you bring the clipboard too. Gaby said we have to report back on the performance of these toys."

Wayne snorted. "Rating on performance is guaranteed to make a guy wilt."

"I'm pretty sure you have nothing to worry about, hotshot." Jen eyed his groin and winked. "You know how to handle the equipment to best advantage."

Sebastian smiled at their banter, pausing in the doorway of Jen's room to watch them until they disappeared from sight. Both of them together and plenty of privacy. He couldn't wait to get started. They needed to focus on Wayne first to help him get it into his stupid head that they wanted him. This was about three people together, not a regular twosome.

He selected the toys and supplies, along with the clipboard, and headed to Wayne's bedroom. He came to a halt in the doorway, watching the two kiss and touch. He waited for a sense of seclusion to hit him, but all he could think was how beautiful they looked together. Jen's creamy complexion contrasted with Wayne's darker coloring, which came courtesy of his Māori heritage. Their hands stroked and wandered over each other in an erotic ballet.

"I don't think I mentioned starting without me," he said, striding up to the bed.

They stopped and stared at him.

"I was cold," Wayne said.

"Huh." Sebastian set the supplies on top of the bedside cabinet and stripped, aware of the interest in their gazes.

"You do that very well," Jen said. "Graceful. Ever thought of trying out for the male strip show that tours

Australasia?"

Wayne barked out a laugh. "He'd get stage fright and wouldn't fill his G-string. No amount of pulling at his dick would put things right."

"Lucky I'm a builder then," Sebastian said. "Jen." He beckoned her over and whispered a couple of suggestions in her ear.

"Good idea," she murmured.

"Should I be worried?" Wayne asked, propping himself up on an elbow.

"Not at all," Jen purred at him. "Lie flat on your back in the middle of the bed."

Wayne followed her order but appeared uncomfortable. Sebastian knew Wayne liked to control the situation. Too bad. This was a good way of showing him they were three people who could live and love in different combinations but together they were even stronger.

"We're going to kiss and tease you a little before we get to the good stuff. Okay?" Sebastian caught Wayne's gaze and didn't release it until he was sure Wayne was willing to submit to their wishes.

"You won't hurt me?"

"Of course not. Why would you think that?" Jen pressed a lazy kiss to the corner of Wayne's mouth. "Lie back and relax. Close your eyes and let us do the work."

Surprise struck Sebastian when Wayne actually followed Jen's suggestion. They climbed on the bed, one either side of Wayne, and started to kiss him. Much as he and Wayne had done to Jen down by the river. Slow sips of his mouth, and the odd three-way kiss. They took their time, with leisurely tastes and licks, unworried about interruptions this time.

As in their river dalliance, a connection slipped into place, making every touch and taste, every kiss feel that much sweeter. Sebastian nibbled his way down Wayne's neck, tasting the faint saltiness of Wayne's skin. Jen murmured a faint sound of contentment, and Sebastian understood exactly how she felt. This was right on so many levels.

Gradually they moved down Wayne's body. Judging by Wayne's erection, he was enjoying the hell out of this too. They lingered, teasing every inch of Wayne's skin, deliberately bypassing his groin region until they'd stirred him to moans. That was their signal to move in for the kill.

Sebastian wondered how he'd deal with licking his best friend's cock. A few weeks ago the mere thought would have filled him with horror. Yes, he'd wanted more from Wayne but he hadn't let himself think too much about the specifics. A silent laugh rumbled in his chest. How would Wayne deal with the physical contact? Hopefully

Jen's presence would help to hold back the weirdness.

Sebastian traced the curve of a thigh muscle and silently signaled Jen. Together they licked along Wayne's shaft, their mouths sealing in a kiss when they reached the tip, tracing Wayne's cock head between their lips.

A startled grunt came from Wayne, but he didn't jerk away from the contact. When Sebastian glanced sideways, he saw Wayne watching them avidly, the glint of arousal shining in his eyes. Sebastian deliberately stroked his tongue over the flared head of Wayne's cock.

"Hell." Wayne groaned and encouraged, Sebastian repeated the move, tasting a hint of pre-cum this time.

Sebastian continued to play and silently challenge Wayne. To his great pleasure, Wayne didn't hold back his feelings. He started speaking, interspersing words with groans.

"That feels good," Wayne whispered.

His body tensed and his hips jerked whenever Sebastian or Jen hit exactly the right spot.

Sebastian lifted his head. "Jen, it's time."

She raised her head, offering Sebastian a sweet smile. "I'm looking forward to this." She reached over and grabbed the smallest butt plug. It also contained a vibrator, and Sebastian knew from experience exactly how good it felt once he'd stopped worrying about having something shoved up his arse. Jen picked up the lube.

Wayne took one look and paled, so Sebastian decided it was time to offer a distraction. He grasped Wayne's cock and ran his tongue along the length. When he reached the head, he took it into his mouth, moving slowly so as not to startle Wayne.

Their gazes caught and something tightened inside Sebastian. *This*. This connection was exactly what he'd dreamed about yet hadn't quite known how to pull it off. He used his tongue, teasing. Giving Wayne a hint of teeth to shove him into a bit of a panic. He must have been doing something right because the stream of pre-cum continued. Sebastian took his time, experimenting and doing everything to Wayne that he enjoyed, never taking his focus off Wayne the entire time.

Wayne's hips jolted and Sebastian grinned around his cock, not letting up on the stimulation, yet keeping it slow and easy. Jen was obviously doing her stuff.

Sebastian watched the emotions flow over his friend's face—the uncertainty. The pleasure. And finally, the slow relaxation that denoted acceptance.

A metallic buzz pierced Sebastian's awareness. Wayne shuddered, driving his cock deeper into Sebastian's mouth. His gag reflex kicked in, and Sebastian lifted his head.

"You okay, Wayne?"

"Gonna come soon."

Jen switched the vibrator off and Wayne grunted.

"If this scenario was meant to give me blue balls then it's working."

"Multi-choice. You can fuck Jen missionary style and she can suck me off at the same time or Jen can ride you and you can suck me off." Sebastian was aware he'd tensed, yet he couldn't help it. If Wayne rejected him this way he wasn't sure how he'd deal.

"Second one," Wayne said after a long enough hesitation to make Sebastian nervous. "Not sure I can swallow though."

The relief made Sebastian giddy. "No problem. I don't know if I can either."

"I can swallow," Jen said with a trace of smugness. "It's no big deal once you get used to the texture. It's like doing shots of whiskey without the afterburn." As she spoke, she straddled Wayne's hips and rolled a condom onto him. With the condom in place, she guided Wayne to her entrance and sank down.

"Damn, that looks hot," Wayne said, his gaze caught by the sight of his shaft disappearing into Jen's body.

Sebastian couldn't tear his eyes away, totally agreeing with Wayne. He watched Jen rise up again, her juices making Wayne's dick shine in the late afternoon light.

Wayne's usual smart grin was back. "I could watch that all day. Come up here so I can reach you."

Sebastian swallowed, both excited and apprehensive at the same time. "Are you sure you want to do this?"

"You did it for me. Works both ways."

Sebastian moved up the bed, his balls starting to throb when Sebastian pictured the process. The flash of tongue. The tight fit of a warm mouth. The graze of teeth.

Wayne went straight for the kill, taking Sebastian's cock deep and sucking at the same time. His tongue caressed Sebastian, dragging across his flesh. Sebastian hissed, the sharp pleasure ripping through him once he realized Wayne wasn't just going through the motions. He seemed to be enjoying the process.

"Turn on the vibrator again," Sebastian ordered Jen.

After fumbling briefly, she managed to flip the switch. Wayne's mouth went slack for an instant before he fought for control. His mouth tightened again, sealing heat around a large portion of Sebastian's cock.

"Watch Jen," Sebastian whispered, turning his body a fraction so he could follow his suggestion.

Jen rode Wayne slowly, her eyes closed and head thrown back. A single finger teased at her clit, smoothing her juices around the swollen nub and every third or fourth stroke

156

she went for direct contact. A loud gasp came from her, her back arched and her finger slid back and forth in urgent strokes.

"I love a woman who knows exactly what she wants," Wayne murmured, after releasing Sebastian's cock. "Damn, I can feel her pussy clutching my cock."

"Suck me harder," Sebastian said. "Take me as deep as you can then flick your tongue along the underside."

A grunt escaped Wayne. "Fuck," he muttered, the cords of his neck tensing. "I don't know if I can concentrate on all that with this thing buzzing in my arse."

"Blood pooled in your dick," Sebastian taunted.

"See how you go with a woman squeezing the life out of your cock."

"Not a competition, boys." She reached behind her, her weight shifting. Wayne's eyes rolled. He cursed, his eyes squeezing tightly shut, and he came, his orgasm ripping through him.

Fearful of an injury, Sebastian jerked away, winging an affronted scowl at Jen when she dared to laugh. Gradually, Wayne relaxed and his eyes opened.

"Jen, turn the vibrator off. Please. I don't think I can take much more."

Sebastian palmed his cock, frustration making him crabby.

"Knock that off. Shit, that feels better. Jen, come up here and give me instructions about this swallowing business."

"You don't have to do that," Sebastian protested.

"I want to," Wayne said. "Besides, if I can do it then you'll want to do it for me. I like the idea of you on your hands and knees."

"Asshole," Sebastian muttered, for form only. Wayne's words brought a surge of happiness. He'd known this was the right way to approach Wayne's insecurities. That and not letting him attend any family outings alone. Sebastian had a standing invitation but he didn't always go because, even though they didn't mean to, they made him feel like an outsider.

Wayne sucked him down, the heat still taking Sebastian by surprise. Wayne wasn't gentle or tentative. In fact he veered toward roughness, yet his touch felt exactly right. Jen whispered in Wayne's ear, and the next thing Sebastian had a lubed finger up his arse. Two perfect strokes of that finger along with the hard draw of Wayne's mouth, and he lost the fragile control he held over his body. He came in hard, explosive contractions, sparks igniting in his groin and ripping across his nerve endings.

Wayne grunted and pulled back, receiving a blast of semen in his face.

An appalled groan burst from Sebastian. "Sorry, man.

My control is shot."

Wayne grinned and wiped his face with the corner of the sheet. "I thought I did pretty well."

"Big head," Sebastian said when he could breathe again. After removing condoms and toys and cleaning up, they lay on the bed in a pile of sweaty bodies. Sebastian had never felt happier.

THE FIRST DAY OF school was even worse than she'd imagined. From the moment she stepped into the classroom, the other students stared. Even the teacher showed extraordinary interest in her presence. Face aflame, she offered a bright smile and picked up her pen to focus on taking notes. Give it a week and they'd become used to her presence. Soon she'd blend in—apart from the uniform. As an adult student, the headmistress said she wasn't required to wear a uniform, but the lack made her stick out. She made a mental note to buy a couple of skirts and trousers in the same dark color as the other students' uniforms. That way a glance wouldn't single her out as different.

Soon her head hurt from all the facts thrown at them, and her butt ached in sympathy. She wasn't used to sitting for such long stretches of time.

Lunch was a lonely sandwich, eaten outdoors in the sun. Why had returning to school been such a great idea?

Education is important. Promise me you'll return to school when you can.

Her mother's words echoed through her head. Determined. Implacable. Jen could still feel the tight pinch of her mother's fingers as she'd gripped Jen's arm, insistent on getting her daughter to understand.

Promise me you'll return to school, Jen, and go to university. Everyone needs a qualification to get ahead.

A sigh whispered from Jen as she studied the groups of students around the school grounds. No matter how uncomfortable, she couldn't go back on her promise to her mother. It was a matter of pride.

And the fact that her mother would probably return from the grave and haunt her if she didn't carry out her pledge.

Just after four, Jen dragged her bag of books from her car and trudged into the house. Even though she didn't feel like it, she dumped her pack on a chair and pulled out her books. If she did all her homework as soon as she arrived home she'd have her evenings free to veg out with her men.

She froze, her hand gripping a heavy chemistry tome.

Her men?

No, no, no!

She'd be leaving to attend university in Auckland next year. This thing with Wayne and Sebastian was about fun. That was all.

That's right! Her mother's voice echoed through her head. Just as well she hadn't spoken up the previous evening in the midst of their lovemaking.

Jen made a cup of coffee and started work, only pausing to prepare a chicken for dinner. She shoved it into the preheated oven, ready to tackle her last assignment—reading several pages from the chemistry book.

Wayne's deep voice echoed from the front door. "Hi, honey. We're home."

"Something smells good," Sebastian said from the doorway. "You didn't have to start dinner."

"It wasn't a problem." Jen couldn't help smiling at the pleasure on Sebastian's face. Starting dinner was such a small thing.

Sebastian wrapped his arms around her, hugging her tight and pressing a kiss on the top of her head. "It's good to have you here at the end of a work day." Sincerity laced his words, prompting curiosity in her.

"Ugh! Sweaty." She struggled and, grinning, he released her.

She knew that he and Wayne had met at a foster home and that Wayne had left to join a family while Sebastian had remained in the foster system until age eighteen. He'd never had a proper home, she thought in enlightenment. It might have been just her and her mother, but her mother had gone out of her way to build a cozy, secure place for them both.

"Do we need to do anything to help?" Wayne asked.

"You both look as if you need a shower," she said, reaching over to pluck a chunk of sawdust from Wayne's hair. "And you're very stinky," she added, kissing the tip of Sebastian's nose to soften her remarks. She blew a kiss to Wayne. "Go take a shower and I'll take care of the rest of dinner."

They stomped down the passage toward the bathroom, although how men could make so much noise wearing just their socks was beyond her. She checked the jacket potatoes and removed them from the oven. After whipping up a quick gravy, she placed the salad on the table and popped some pre-cooked dinner rolls into the oven to finish cooking. Masculine laughter came from the bathroom and a frisson of heat danced down her spine when she imagined their naked bodies beaded with droplets of water. She fanned the heat from her face with a swish of her hand.

"Hey," she yelled. "No hanky-panky without me."

"Spoilsport," Wayne shouted back.

Five minutes later the two men strolled into the kitchen.

"That's better," she said with approval. "You can kiss me properly now."

Eyes gleaming, they advanced on her, corralling her with male heat and muscles. Firm lips met hers while another set of lips nibbled on the delicate flesh of her neck. Her nipples pulled tight and heat bloomed in her sex, mere seconds after their touch. It was as if her body were programmed to react to them. She certainly wanted them both.

"You smell good." Emotion darkened Sebastian's eyes. "I'm glad you're here."

His words sank in, twisting strands of confusion through her. This living situation could only be temporary until she left for Auckland. Call her old-fashioned but she didn't think long distance relationships worked. "We'd better eat dinner before it gets cold." Huh! Neat sidestep. Avoiding thinking about the situation wasn't going to change the truth. She couldn't let herself think of Wayne and Sebastian as anything more than good friends because her future was at stake, her promise to her mother.

"How was school?" Wayne asked.

"Horrid."

Sebastian pulled out a chair and seated her. "Why is

that?"

"My classmates are so young. They've known each other for a long time because they've gone through the classes together, many of them since kindergarten. I stand out like the flock of red sheep in Ted Morrison's front yard."

A chuckle burst from Wayne. "Why did Morrison dye his sheep that color anyway?"

"Someone paid him," Jen said. "It was an advertising stunt for the local radio station."

"So school isn't that great?" Sebastian's face bore sympathy.

Jen sighed, her stomach churning at the reminder of her day. "I'm sure it will get better. Heck, I knew it wouldn't be easy."

"Nothing worth doing is easy," Wayne said.

Sebastian groaned. "Your mother always used to say that."

"Still does," Wayne said. "I topped up on parental advice during the weekend. Need to pass it on. Get it out of my head somehow."

Jen happened to be watching Sebastian, saw his shift of expression. She'd seen it before—usually when someone was talking about their family. Interesting. Sebastian wasn't easy to read, yet in this she could practically see the words on the page.

Wayne cocked his head and studied her with sympathy. "Two of my brothers are still at school. Do you want me to ask them to—?"

"No! Maybe it will be better once I get to know the rest of the students and the teachers."

"Say that once more with confidence," Wayne ordered.

"It will be better in a few weeks." Jen sucked in a deep breath and held up crossed fingers.

Chapter Ten

Two weeks later

"I WANT YOU TO divide into threes for this assignment," the teacher said, almost as soon as she walked to the front of the classroom. "Collectively you'll do a report on how some aspect of Sloan could be improved. You can do it in movie format or use a power point presentation or any other media available to you. You have a month to complete the assignment. Each group will hand in their assignment to me and present them to the rest of the class at a later date."

Every student groaned, Jen included. This was gonna be fun.

"I'll give you five minutes to organize your groups. If you're undecided by that time, I will make an executive decision."

Great. It was like a sports day all over again. She'd be the last one picked.

The rest of the students burst into chatter. Jen cast a cautious glance to her left and another to her right. She caught the gaze of the gum-chewing girl sitting at the next desk. "Would you like to work with me?"

The gum snapped as she shifted it around her mouth. "Nah, I have a group already."

Jen nodded, holding her breath when the backs of her eyes started to sting. She would not cry. *She would not.*

She was an adult and could get past a stupid thing like an assignment. She looked the other way and saw that the girl sitting there was obviously in a group. The one in front too.

"Righto! Quiet everyone." The teacher clapped her hands together. "Melanie, take that gum out of your mouth right now."

The gum snapping came to an abrupt halt.

"Does anyone not have a group?"

Jen stuck up her hand, but she was the only one.

"Gerrard, who is in your group?"

"Justin and Stan."

"Right," the teacher said. "Jen can join your group. Maybe she can keep you in line."

Jen didn't want to keep three teenage boys under control. She seethed while she feverishly scribbled notes of some of the things the teacher required covered in the project. At the end of the class she waited to approach the teacher. The group of boys who'd had her foisted on them beat her to the complaint.

"We don't want a girl in our group."

"What's wrong with a girl?" Jen demanded.

The boy opened his mouth, unsure now that she'd confronted him directly.

"They giggle," one of his friends said.

Jen still hadn't managed to match names and faces for the entire class, so she wasn't clear on his identity.

"I'm sure Jen is mature enough to restrain her giggling," the teacher said drily. "She's new and needs help to blend in a bit more. The three of you are popular and will help her with that."

Okaaay.

That sort of burst Jen's argument. The teacher had noticed her difficulties and was trying to help.

"And the three of you together are trouble," the teacher continued. "You're all intelligent, and I intend you to pass this year."

No doubting the determination in her steady gaze.

"Why don't I give you my phone number and you guys can ring me tonight?" Jen said, flashing her smile again. Damn, her jaw was starting to ache with all her friendly overtures. She pulled a notepad and pen from the side pocket of her pack and scribbled down her cell number and the number for Wayne's place.

The rest of her school day progressed as usual. Jen stuck on her own with the other students pretending to ignore her, yet watching her closely and whispering to each other when they thought she wouldn't notice.

"School any better today?" Wayne asked, walking into the kitchen where she was doing her homework.

"Where's Sebastian?"

"He had to drive to Auckland to see a bathroom supplier. They're stuffin' us around, and we wanted to get a face-to-face meeting. And you didn't answer my question. School?"

"It sucked. In one of my classes we have group assignments, and the teacher stuck me with three boys."

Wayne blinked. His lips twitched, and her eyes narrowed in return.

"Don't laugh at me."

"I thought you liked boys," Wayne said.

"Not teenage ones," she muttered and barely suppressed a shudder. "They're not civilized."

"Nearly finished your homework?"

"Yeah. Pour me a glass of wine in five minutes."

"I had something else in mind."

"Yeah?"

"Oh yeah." Wayne grinned and hauled her off her chair. He wrapped his arms around her. When their lips met, her knees went weak, and she clutched his shoulders letting the passion wash over her. He stoked the emotions with each aggressive kiss of her lips and the more subtle stroke of his tongue.

"Hey, Wayne. Wayne!"

Wayne muttered an oath against her neck and loosened his grip but didn't let her go. It wasn't difficult to guess why since his erection butted against her stomach.

"What are you doing here? You didn't think to knock?" He glared at the three young men standing in the kitchen doorway.

Jen felt the color spread across her face, and mumbled the same curse Wayne had muttered under her breath. "I told you to ring. How did you know where I live?"

Wayne's brown eyes narrowed. "You know each other?"

"They're in my class, and we're working on an assignment together," Jen said.

"I recognized the phone number," Gerrard replied, his brows drawn together as he stared at the pair of them.

Wayne barked out a sudden laugh. "Meet my brother Gerrard and his friends Stan and Justin."

"We've met," Jen said faintly. "I didn't know he was your brother." They didn't look anything alike, despite

170

both having Māori blood. Gerrard's features were broader and he didn't have the same lazy confidence Wayne bore, although that would probably come with age and experience.

"We have different surnames since we were both adopted." Wayne's amusement was obvious now. He pressed a quick kiss to her mouth and released her. "I'll grab a shower and leave you guys to discuss your assignment."

"Would you like something to drink?" Jen grabbed for her polite hostess-mode to help relieve her embarrassment.

"We'll have a beer," Gerrard said.

"No you won't," Wayne shouted from the hall. "Mum would skin me alive."

"I'm drinking ginger beer," Jen said. "Will that work?"

Justin nodded. "Sure."

"Have a seat." Jen grabbed three extra glasses and filled them with ice. She added ginger beer and placed them on the table. That done, she took a deep breath and sat with the three teenage boys, feeling a little more in control. She rifled through her notes and pulled out the ones she'd taken relating to the assignment they needed to complete.

"Are you Wayne's girlfriend?"

Her head jerked up to find the three boys scrutinizing her.

"So are you?" Gerrard repeated his question.

Jen swallowed. It was that simple yet complicated as well because of Sebastian. "Yes," she said, opting for simplicity.

Gerrard nodded, and in that brief moment it was easy to see he idolized Wayne. And because of Wayne, she'd found an *in* with Gerrard and his friends.

"Do you always do your homework when you get home from school?" Justin asked, wrinkling his freckled nose.

"Yes because that way it's done and I have the rest of the night or weekend to do the things I'd rather do."

"I hadn't thought of that," Stan said.

"Maybe I might try your idea. If Mum sees me doing my homework she might not make me help with dinner," Gerrard commented.

Jen stifled a laugh. "It might work."

"What should we do for the assignment?" Stan asked.

They tossed around one or two ideas, finally settling on one they thought had good possibilities.

"We should make a video," Gerrard said.

"And set up a page on the social media to get more information and contact people who are interested in our topic."

Their enthusiasm surprised Jen. Her pen flew across the page as she took notes of the things they decided to action. She couldn't help but be excited about their project.

Wayne returned and topped up their drinks before starting on dinner. "What time is Mum expecting you home?"

"I told her we'd be back by six."

Wayne nodded. "You'd better keep an eye on the time then."

"Stan and Justin are staying the night and going with us to the agricultural show tomorrow. We want to see the monster trucks."

"Sounds good. I might take Jen if she wants to go," Wayne said. "Next time ring before you arrive and knock. Don't come in until one of us answers the door."

Gerrard smirked. "In case we interrupt at a bad time."

"Exactly," Wayne said, his tone and expression stern.

Jen didn't know where to look when the three boys sniggered. Once again, her wretched propensity for blushing made her discomfort clear.

The boys left half an hour later, all piling into Stan's old, beat-up car.

"They like you," Wayne said, wrapping his arms around her and nuzzling her neck.

"Only because they discovered I'm not only living here, but I'm your girlfriend."

"It's not just that, Jen. You listened to their ideas and didn't try to take over because you're older. You treated them like contemporaries."

Jen snorted. "They know way more than me when it comes to this stuff. I've never had time to play around with social media and the things these kids take for granted. It's like navigating a new world. Believe me, they're helping me more than I'm aiding them." But despite her words, she was quietly pleased about their progress. The boys had treated her like an equal. It would be interesting to see if this carried on when they returned to school on Monday.

Wayne checked his watch. "Sebastian should be back soon. Why don't we open a bottle of wine while we wait for him?"

"I thought we were going to mess around?"

A cheeky grin lit up his face. "Hold that thought. Dinner won't be long. Besides, I want to fool around with Sebastian too."

Sebastian arrived not long after they'd opened a bottle of merlot. "Man, the traffic in Auckland was a real bitch. I think everyone was leaving the city for the weekend."

"Would a kiss make it better?" Wayne asked.

Sebastian's gaze zoomed in on Wayne's mouth before sliding to view hers. A tingle sprang to life in Jen, a zip of excitement darting to her pussy. "I'll need more than one kiss to forget the hellish traffic."

Wayne chuckled and rose smoothly from his chair. He

rounded the kitchen table and hauled Sebastian into his arms, drawing him closer for a kiss. Jen watched avidly, never ceasing to feel amazed at the arousal that filled her whenever she watched them. They always started aggressively, each struggling to take control. The first kiss was a clash of lips, a fierce groan and tight, gripping hands. Then the violence fled. Their contact gentled, lips softened and sexy moans of pleasure escaped them.

Unbidden, Jen stood, following the silent urge to join them. She clasped Sebastian's biceps and tugged to gain his attention. "My turn."

Wayne laughed and moved a fraction to let her squish between him and Sebastian. When she lifted her head for Sebastian's kiss, Wayne moved in behind her. She practically felt the connection slip into place. Each time they came together, the ties binding them seemed to grow and become more. Right now there wasn't anywhere else she'd rather be. Sebastian started the kiss slow before taking it into carnal territory. He stroked along her tongue and then the roof of her mouth. She sighed and squirmed closer, physical need creeping through her body. She felt her nipples prickle and the heaviness between her thighs increased.

"Hold that thought." Wayne stepped away from her and lightly slapped her backside. "I'll heat the barbeque and put on the steaks."

"It's very warm in here." Sebastian traced one blunt finger along the neckline of her cotton shirt. A raft of goose bumps rose on her skin when he repeated the touch. "You should take this off."

"You'd like that, wouldn't you?" Jen asked in a dry voice.

"Hell, yes. It's a recent fantasy. I want to see you eating your dinner topless."

"Oh?" Somehow when Sebastian made the suggestion it sounded tempting instead of sleazy.

"Or better yet, I'd like her naked on top of the table. We could use her as a plate," Wayne said.

"Only if you guys take a turn as well," Jen said firmly.

"Deal," said Sebastian.

"What?" She stared at Sebastian before turning to Wayne. "You're not serious!"

"Very serious, but I think we'll save it for dessert," Wayne said. "I wouldn't like you to get burned."

"No," Jen agreed.

"We'll take a turn too. You go tonight. I'll go tomorrow night and Wayne can have Sunday night."

"All of a sudden I'm looking forward to dessert," Wayne said.

"The pair of you are nuts if you think I'm going to stretch out on the top of that table naked and let the pair of you treat me like a plate."

But the two men talked a good game, and after eating her dinner and drinking two glasses of wine, she found herself stripping.

"This is where I do my homework," she protested faintly as they helped her to climb up on top of the table. "How am I meant to do—"

"Stop arguing," Sebastian said in a firm voice.

"At least draw the curtains so no one can see inside."

"We'll hear any visitors before they have a chance to peek," Wayne said.

"You didn't hear your brother's arrival. He walked into the house and spoke before we heard him."

"I'll lock the door, if it will make you feel better," Sebastian said, leaving to carry out his promise. On his return, he drew the curtains across the windows leading out to the deck. "I'll light some candles. Make it more romantic," he said in a rough voice.

It was the perfect thing to help relax her. With the curtains and the locked door giving privacy, some of the tension in her dissipated. The flicker of candles and the cinnamon scent they gave off did the rest.

"Here's a pillow." Sebastian tucked it under her head and smoothed a hand over her shoulder. "You okay?"

Jen swallowed. "Yes."

"Good." Sebastian's eyes gleamed, even in the candlelight. His hand moved down her arm and strayed to her breast. He tweaked her nipple, pinching again when she groaned. "Wayne, what's for dessert?"

"I was thinking I'd barbeque fruit and serve it with ice cream, but we can have fresh fruit instead."

"Ice cream," Jen said. "That sounds cold."

"Don't worry. By the time we're finished with you, your skin will sizzle so hot you'll need the ice cream to cool you down."

"Huh."

"She doesn't believe you," Wayne said, producing a can of whipped cream and a plate of diced fruit.

"Do we have any chocolate topping left?"

"There's a new bottle in the pantry." Wayne shook the can of cream and pulled off the lid.

A spurt of excitement shot through her. Being the center of attention was like an aphrodisiac. Two sets of eyes looking at her with lust and desire. Four hands placing cubes of fruit on her, touching her with teasing fingers. Two mouths to do decadent things to her trembling body.

Oh yeah. It was good being her right at this minute.

Wayne sprayed whipped cream over her in swirls. Not just random patterns, but indulging the artist inside him, he fashioned a work of art, one resembling his tattoo.

"Nice," Sebastian said with admiration. "You need to design one for me."

"You'd get a tattoo, something that I designed?"

"It would be a way of showing how much I'm committed to you and Jen," Sebastian said.

Jen watched her two men, a lump forming in her throat. Once again Wayne was easier to read than Sebastian, but she was starting to understand them both better. She caught the flash of pleasure in Sebastian. The honesty, and then it faded into a sexy smile.

"If I get a tattoo, then maybe Jen should get one. Maybe a small one on your hip just for us to see."

"A brand?"

"Just like a brand," Wayne said with a growl of approval.

"I didn't realize the two of you were so possessive." It didn't seem the right time to remind them that she'd be leaving next year. She liked spending time with Sebastian and Wayne, liked the way they treated her, but she couldn't allow herself to fall in love with them.

"You'd better believe it," Sebastian said.

Wayne picked up one of her hands and pressed a tender kiss to her inner wrist. "You make us happy." He dropped her hand and picked up the chocolate sauce. With it, he formed intricate patterns on the cream on her torso while Sebastian busied himself with bits of fruit, decorating her. He paused to feed her a slice of juicy peach, the tart sweetness sliding over her taste buds as she bit down.

Sebastian watched her avidly, groaning when a trickle of peach juice dribbled from the corner of her mouth. He bent over and delicately licked it away. Her breath caught, and she wanted to drag him closer and seduce him with kisses and erotic touches.

"No! Don't move. Finished," Wayne said, setting both the chocolate syrup and the cream aside.

Sebastian drew back to stare, his gaze roving her slowly, his eyes dark with stormy passion. "Would you let us take a photo?"

Her heart gave a sudden thump. Did she trust them enough? She waited for them to rush in and reassure her, to say they'd never share an intimate photo with their friends. But neither said a word. A direct contrast with the time Giles had tried to talk her into a home movie. She glanced down her body. It wasn't as if there was much of her visible. Her chest heaved when she sucked in a breath. "All right."

"One photo each," Sebastian said, picking up his phone.

"And you can take a photo of me and Seb kissing," Wayne said. "I know how hot that makes you."

"Deal," Jen said, every last bit of apprehension leaving her. Without much fuss they'd understood how much trust a photo entailed, and in return they were showing her that they trusted her too. For a moment the emotion swelling in her chest seemed too big for her to contain. It pushed up her throat and she had to swallow several times.

Sebastian snapped a shot with his phone camera, approval showing in the way he reached for her hand and gave it a gentle squeeze.

"Smile," Wayne said, and he clicked a shot too before setting his phone aside. "Now where were we?"

"Want a strawberry, Jen?" Sebastian picked up a large, glossy red berry and swirled it across the curve of her breast. She tingled at the contact, a wave of warmth suffusing her as she watched him bite into the ripe berry. He smacked his lips and dipped his head to lick around the same breast. His tongue tickled as he cleaned away a trail of chocolate syrup. "Delicious."

Sebastian fed her a slice of nectarine while Wayne feasted on her other breast. When he lifted his head, cream and chocolate decorated his mouth and chin. His tongue flickered out and some of the cream disappeared.

"Let me," Sebastian said in a hoarse voice. He grabbed Wayne and licked away the last of the chocolate. "Tastes much better eaten off skin."

"You go on that side, and I'll stay on this side of the table," Wayne said.

"That way you can kiss each other too," Jen said.

As usual, watching the two men interact had a predictable effect on her body. The two men fed her and each other pieces of fruit, gradually removing the cream and chocolate to uncover skin beneath. They worked down her body, each lick and brush of fingers stoking the desire within Jen. Distinct dampness pooled between her thighs, and she longed for them to reach the good bits.

"Just as well you're not ticklish," Wayne whispered.

Sebastian kissed her hipbone. "I'm sorry we've finished dessert. That was very appetizing."

"Not quite finished," Wayne said. "Part your legs for us."

"So pretty," Sebastian said, idly trailing his fingers over her upper thigh while he studied her pussy. "She's all pink and swollen."

"Look how wet she is. She liked us touching her." Wayne caressed her clit, the touch featherlight.

A tremor zapped Jen. "Please make me come."

"Our pleasure," Sebastian purred.

Wayne parted her legs a fraction more and both he and Sebastian started to lick. They laughed when their heads collided, gave a collective groan when they tasted her. Then without verbal communication they concentrated on getting her off. Wayne focused his attention on her clit, stroking and teasing, while Sebastian fucked her with his fingers. Each stroke went in and out. In and out.

"Oh god," Jen muttered. Every time was magical. Being the sole focus of both men—just the thought of it was enough to send her flying. The reality propelled her into orbit. A moan slipped free. She bit down on her bottom lip, trying to hold back the surge of pleasure threatening to sweep her away. But it was too much. Too big. A drag of a tongue over her sweet spot and a thrust of a finger and climax crashed over her. Huge waves dragged her under into a place where only sensation ruled. She gasped, feeling shattered yet weightless and so happy she could burst.

Chapter Eleven

Six weeks later

JEN WOKE UP ALONE. She patted the bed each side of her, groping for a warm male body. It took her a few seconds to remember that Sebastian and Wayne had started early in a push to complete their current contract before the due date. Wayne wanted to have a romantic weekend away, and Sebastian had agreed, sweeping her along with his enthusiasm. All going well they were off to Queenstown in the South Island for a romantic break where they didn't have to hide or worry about local gossip.

The alarm went off, the strident demand for her to wake bringing forth a curse. She staggered from bed and sniffed. Her head ached and her stomach roiled. Damn, she couldn't afford to get sick, not with exams coming next week.

After a maths class, she joined Gerrard, Stan and Justin, during morning break. They sat outside, enjoying a quick ten minutes of sunshine before their next class forced them inside again.

Justin blew his nose. Seconds later Stan sneezed, spraying her and Gerrard.

"Damn, Stan," Gerrard muttered. "I don't want the flu."

"I think it's too late for me," Jen said. "I've felt dreadful all morning."

"We can't miss exams," Justin said. "We've never studied so much. I want to make my mother proud when she sees my results."

"You'd better tell Wayne that the other kids gave you the flu. He doesn't need any ideas in his head about us kissing," Gerrard said.

Jen barked out a laugh then sneezed. She dragged a packet of tissues out of her bag and handed Stan some before wiping her own nose. "He trusts me. He knows I don't fool around."

"I wish I could say the same for her." Justin scowled in the direction of a group of giggling girls.

"Her loss," Jen said. "Concentrate on your exams and beat her out of the top of the class spot. That will piss her off more."

"Yeah," Stan agreed. "Especially if we all beat her ass."

"We will," Jen said. "I intend to earn a scholarship for

varsity. Failure is not an option."

The bell went and they wandered back to class. Jen prayed for the weekend to come because she felt like crap.

"Do you want to go out to the Cricket for dinner tonight?" Sebastian made the offer to Wayne and Jen even though he didn't want to go to the pub. He preferred it when they were at home, and he could touch Jen and Wayne without worrying about what other people might think.

Jen sneezed and grabbed for a tissue. "Nah, I've caught the flu that's going around school. I'm gonna have an early night."

Sebastian shared a concerned glance with Wayne. "Do you want something for dinner?"

"No." She swallowed, the color seeping from her face before she took off at a run.

"Shit," Wayne said. "She really is sick. I'll see if I can do anything." He disappeared, only to return a few minutes later. In the distance, a door slammed.

"Is she okay?"

"Grumpy. After spewing up her guts, she told me to piss off and leave her alone. Then she went into her bedroom."

"And slammed the door," Sebastian said. "Let's leave her alone for a while. With any luck she'll go to sleep."

"She's been pushing herself, studying for exams."

Sebastian grabbed a couple of beers from the fridge and handed one to Wayne. "Getting a qualification means a lot to her."

"But what about next year?" Wayne asked. "I get the feeling she's intending to move to Auckland and leave us behind."

Sebastian's gut bucked at the thought. For the first time in years, he felt happy. Secure. Jen's leaving would destroy everything. Hell, it would rip apart his heart as well. He loved Jen. "We'll have to think of a way to compromise because I don't intend to let her go without a fight."

Wayne nodded, his normal carefree mien absent for once. "She could commute if she wanted too."

"It would make the day long, especially if she had to drive in the traffic."

"Depends on her class schedule. Some days are shorter than others," Wayne said. "Maybe she could commute with other people. Share expenses and driving."

"It might work or we could buy an apartment in Auckland. We have to drive up quite a bit to visit suppliers anyway."

Wayne nodded. "That's not a bad idea. Something to

think about."

Sebastian twisted the top off his beer. "It's good to think about this now. We'll have a solid argument if Jen tries to dump us."

A sneeze echoed in the distance.

"I hope we don't catch that," Wayne said.

"If you do, I'm sending you home to your mother. You're a real baby when you're sick."

"You'd miss me." Wayne smirked. "No one to warm your feet on. And speaking of my mother, I promised her I'd drop in and help Dad with some heavy lifting around the garden. If it's okay with you, I might go now then we have the rest of the weekend to ourselves."

"Go. I'll keep an eye on Jen."

"Do you think she needs to go to the doctor?"

"Maybe. We'll see how she is tomorrow morning."

Wayne pushed away from the counter he was leaning on and set his empty bottle on the top. "Call me if you need anything." He advanced on Sebastian and pulled him in for a quick kiss before grabbing his keys and sauntering away."

"Nice arse," Sebastian called.

Wayne laughed and kept walking. "Later, Seb."

Sebastian made a quick sandwich and ate it before going to check on Jen. He paused outside her closed door to listen. When he couldn't hear anything, he carefully opened the door and peered inside. Jen was asleep, face pressed in her pillow, a muffled snore coming from her open mouth. Smiling, he closed the door again. The sleep would do her good. She'd been working extra hard and combined with the flu, it had knocked her out.

He returned to the kitchen, and sent Wayne a text to let him know Jen was sleeping.

As he tidied the kitchen and checked through the mail for the day, he realized this was the first time he'd been alone for ages. He paused, tensing a fraction. The black dog of depression hadn't stalked him for months, not since he'd hooked up with Jen and Wayne. Even now a sense of happiness filled him, a belief in the future. He was building a family, no matter how unconventional. Now he fit in a way he never had before. He belonged, and the feeling was all he'd hoped it would be during his lonely years of growing up without a family.

"When are we going to meet your girlfriend? Bring her to your father's birthday party next week." Wayne's mother beamed. "She sounds like a lovely girl. Gerrard talks about her all the time."

Alarm stirred in the pit of Wayne's stomach. He didn't think introducing Jen to his mother was a good idea. And what about Sebastian? The last thing he wanted to do was push Seb into the background. "I don't know. I—"

"I want to meet the woman who has put the sparkle in your eyes," his mother said firmly. "She has been such a good influence on Gerrard and his friends. You invite her. I expect to meet her the Sunday after next."

"Sure, Mum." Wayne gave up trying to argue. "Can Sebastian come too?"

"As long as he doesn't bring one of those dreadful girls."

Irritation started a slow simmer, and he bit back a retort. As much as he loved his mother, she'd never been more than lukewarm toward Sebastian. He could never figure out why, although he'd noted his mother's approval rating was higher with friends who had Māori or Island ancestors. Certainly all his adopted brothers and sisters bore Māori blood. "Sebastian won't be bringing a date."

Two of his sisters walked into the kitchen. Even though they weren't blood related, with their long, dark hair and similar heights, they could have passed as twins.

"Are you bringing the girl who Gerrard keeps talking about?" Marie asked.

Janie grinned. "I think Gerrard is half in love with her himself."

"I'll ask her," Wayne said.

"Did she grow up in Sloan?" his mother asked.

"Yes. She's lived there most of her life."

"Wayne, are you coming to help or not?" Gerrard yelled from outside.

Saved by the bell. "Coming."

Gerrard spoiled his demand by sneezing and their mother started muttering about mustard plasters. Wayne wouldn't mention that Jen had the flu because he'd suffered through a mustard plaster or two while growing up. He wouldn't want to inflict them on Jen.

As he drove home Wayne thought about the potential problems of taking Jen and Sebastian to his father's birthday party. No matter which way he looked at it, introducing his family to the equation was a big mistake. He, Sebastian and Jen were starting to gel into a unit.

Hell, Jen was still talking about moving to Auckland next year.

Leaving them.

The welcoming lights gleaming from the house eased some of the tension in him. He strode inside, dropping his keys on the counter and heading for the lounge where he heard the low hum of the television.

"Hey." Sebastian glanced up and smiled. It seemed natural to kiss him hello and drop onto the couch beside him.

"How's Jen?"

"Still sleeping. I checked on her a few minutes ago. Things okay with your parents?"

Wayne sighed. "Gerrard told Mum I have a new girlfriend, and she wants to meet Jen. She wants me to take her to Dad's birthday party." Wayne searched Sebastian's face, saw the quick realization of the problem in his lover's expression.

"Take Jen with you," Sebastian said. "Introduce her to your family. Your parents will love her."

Wayne shook his head, seeing the pain Sebastian was trying to hide. "Mum invited you too."

"I won't be able to touch either you or Jen."

Pain wrenched at Wayne, stealing his breath. His chest rose and fell and he couldn't tear his gaze off Sebastian. "I don't think my parents are ready for an announcement like ours. I don't like to keep secrets but—"

"You don't have to explain. I get it. I'd most likely do the same thing if I had a family. Don't worry about it."

But the situation worried Wayne for the rest of the evening. After checking on Jen, he and Sebastian went to bed. They kissed and jerked each other off. Sebastian fell asleep soon after, but Wayne remained wide-eyed for what seemed like hours.

No matter how he looked at the situation, a ticking bomb came to mind.

BY MONDAY, JEN FELT better and she drove to school prepared to sit the first of her exams.

"It wasn't too bad," Gerrard said when they met up after leaving the exam room.

Jen nodded, her stomach roiling without warning. She swallowed rapidly and breathed carefully through her mouth, and luckily the nausea seemed to settle.

Gerrard let out a huge sneeze, and Justin poked him in the ribs.

"Damn," Gerrard muttered. "I thought I'd shaken this stupid flu. If I cough when I get home Mum will make another mustard plaster for me. The cure is way worse than the flu."

"Is that what the weird smell is?" Stan asked.

Justin sniffed. "I can't smell a thing."

"You're lucky. Think smelly socks and add a bit more," Stan said.

"It's not that bad," Jen said. "Anyone want a drink at the canteen? My shout." Maybe a ginger beer would settle her stomach.

It helped a little and she managed to get through her next exam—chemistry. But on the drive home she had to pull over. She barely got the door open before she vomited.

She groped for her water bottle and swished some water around her mouth. "Damn flu."

Jen drove the rest of the way home without mishap. At least she could sleep in a little tomorrow before she started.

ONE WEEK LATER

Jen sucked in a harsh breath as she fought the nausea tap-dancing through her stomach. She stared into the toilet bowl, helpless as the queasiness rose up and burst from her throat. Her shoulders shook with the force of the convulsions, her throat raw by the time she stopped dry-heaving.

A truth slid into her brain. This wasn't the flu. This was much more.

She was pregnant.

It was the only realistic answer because women didn't go around chucking up for no reason at all.

Satisfied she'd finished throwing up, she dragged herself over to the hand basin and washed her hands and face. Pregnant. She'd ring the doctors' surgery for an appointment—no. A pregnancy kit from the chemist would give her an answer and keep the matter a little more private.

Besides, she needed to go to school this morning. It was just lucky that Sebastian and Wayne were starting work so early and hadn't twigged yet to her constant vomiting.

Foregoing breakfast in favor of dry crackers, she packed her books for school and headed out. On automatic pilot, she got through the day, and on the way home from school, she stopped at the chemist. Ignoring the speculative glance from the woman serving at the counter, she shoved the test into her handbag and left.

Neither Sebastian nor Wayne was at home when she arrived. Thank goodness. This could be a false alarm. She really might have the flu.

It wasn't.

Jen stared at the stick. The result read positive.

Tears started rolling down her face. One after another, they plopped onto her arm. This was going to screw up all her plans for the future.

Chapter Twelve

HECK, CRYING WASN'T GOING to solve a thing. Jen swiped her hand over her eyes and searched through her handbag for some tissues.

"Jen. Are you home?" Sebastian burst into the kitchen. He took one look at her and strode over. "What is it? What's wrong?"

"I'm pregnant." God, even saying it out loud didn't make it sound any better. "Sebastian, I can't have a baby."

Sebastian stood frozen, staring at her as if she sported a pair of horns. Typical.

Jen turned away, intending to retreat to her bedroom.

Sebastian's hand shot out. "Pregnant?"

"Yes, so the test says."

"But how?"

A sharp laugh exploded from her. "Surely you've worked out the how by now?"

"Damn." Sebastian ran a hand through his hair. "Sorry. It's a bit of a shock."

"No kidding!" Another of those stupid tears escaped and she scrubbed at it impatiently.

"Jen, come here."

He opened his arms, and she stumbled into them, the tears falling faster now. She hadn't had time to think about how Sebastian and Wayne would react because she'd been too busy thinking about the upset to her long-term plans. At least Sebastian wasn't angry or wasn't trying to blame her.

"What am I going to do?"

"Don't worry," Sebastian whispered against her hair. "We'll sort something out when Wayne gets home."

"But I won't be able to go to varsity," she wailed.

"Shh, don't worry about that right now." He kissed her neck and held her tighter.

But Sebastian didn't understand. She'd promised her mother. Her attendance at university was for both of them. And as much as she'd loved her mother, she didn't want to relive her life, bringing up a child on her own and working all hours of the day to pay the bills.

"Jen, Wayne and I aren't going to leave you to struggle alone. Surely you know us well enough to understand that."

She pushed away from Sebastian to look up at him. "Sorry. I didn't realize I'd said that out loud."

"You were lumping us into the same category as Giles," Sebastian accused.

"Sorry. I'm still in full panic flight."

"A baby might not be ideal, but it's not the end of everything between us," Sebastian said. "If anything a baby will make us into a tighter unit."

"You're pleased," she said, her voice flat.

"Excited," he agreed. "But I can understand how you feel too. We'll talk when Wayne gets home, make a plan. I'm sure we can think of something to make a baby work for all of us."

Jen sniffed. "I don't see how."

"Ye of little faith." Sebastian tipped up her chin with one forefinger and kissed her on the lips.

At first she didn't respond, but he deepened the kiss, taking it from sweet and tender to something deeper and more personal. He showed her with touch how much he cared until she could do nothing but hold on and kiss him back. Sweet. So sweet and compassionate. Warmth swelled inside her until her entire body hummed with pleasure and all she could think about was Sebastian filling her, fucking her. No! Making love to her. This was lovemaking rather than plain old sex.

Sebastian's hands glided down her back to cup her butt and hold her against him. When he lifted her, the ridge of his cock slotted neatly right where she needed it. A soft mewl of desire whispered from her as she started to fully participate. Their lips slid together and she rubbed against him, trying to get a closer contact.

"What are you doing?"

Jen and Sebastian jerked apart, shocked out of their romantic bubble.

"You're playing around with Sebastian behind Wayne's back." Gerrard's jaw worked, anger distorting his face. "I thought you were his friend." He shook his head, betrayal glimmering in his eyes. "And you—" He cut off abruptly and stomped out of the kitchen. A door slammed and when Jen strained to hear she caught the faint grumble of a car starting.

"Fuck," Sebastian said.

"We weren't doing anything wrong."

"It doesn't matter. What happens if he tells everyone?"

"Wayne will sort it out."

"Like you're both going to fix my pregnancy?" Jen asked, and the tears started flowing again. "I think I'll go and have a shower."

"Do you want me to scrub your back?"

"I want to be alone."

Sebastian nodded and clenched his hands to fists to avoid reaching for her. She looked like a wounded animal, and he felt bad because he wanted to scream his joy to the world. Hell, he didn't even know if he was the father, and he didn't care.

The warm sensation in his chest grew bigger and bigger, and his smile expanded so much his mouth ached with the joy of it. A family.

He heard a vehicle pull up and hurried to the door, recognizing the roar of the engine. He opened the door and stood in the doorway waiting for Wayne.

"Good news. Bad news," he burst out. "Which do you want first?"

"Good. Maybe it will improve my shitty day."

Sebastian's gaze arrowed in on Wayne's T-shirt. "Is that blood? Are you hurt?"

"No, Tommy cut his hand. I had to take him to the doctor. He's okay but he'll be off work for a while."

"Fuck." Tommy was one of their most experienced workers.

"Yeah, so I could do with some good news."

"Jen's pregnant," Sebastian burst out.

"The bad news?"

"Jen was a bit upset, and Gerrard walked in on us. He

thinks Jen is cheating with me."

"Fuck," Wayne muttered. "I need a drink."

"A beer?"

"Nah, break out the strong stuff so I can start working on a hangover."

"Aren't you pleased about the baby?" How could Wayne not be excited?

"I expect Jen isn't pleased. A baby will spoil her plans for her education. Is she going to keep it?"

"Keep it?" Sebastian was aware he was gaping at Wayne. He could see his friend's mouth moving, but he couldn't hear a thing over the roar in his head. Surely Jen wouldn't give up her baby? Have an abortion?

"Sebastian. Sebastian!" Wayne shook him. "Breathe, dammit. Breathe."

Sebastian sucked in a huge breath, Wayne's grip on his biceps helping to ground him, dragging him back from the dark abyss that had opened in his mind. "We need to talk to Jen. She can't give this baby away."

"We will. What did Gerrard say?"

"I think he intends to talk to you."

"Okay. As long as he doesn't go blabbing all over town we can deal with him. If I ask him to he'll keep it quiet."

"But what about Jen?"

Wayne gave him a swift hug before pulling back. "We'll

have to talk to her. It's her body, her future," Wayne said. "We'll have to take her wishes into consideration."

"You mean you'd let her have an abortion?" Shock rippled through Sebastian, knocking down his flimsy defenses until he wanted to yell and lash out with his fists. A low, anguished groan escaped him and he wrenched from Wayne's touch. He had to go. He had to go now before his entire world imploded on him.

Wayne stared after Sebastian, muttered a curse and headed for the booze. He made short work of his first whisky and poured another. Jen pregnant. That wasn't such a big problem for him. He'd do anything Jen wanted even if that meant an abortion because it was Jen's future and well-being that mattered most. Gerrard thinking Sebastian and Jen had betrayed him. That too he could deal with—tomorrow. Gerrard wasn't a blabbermouth. He wouldn't do anything until he'd spoken to Wayne. And he would, because Gerrard was fiercely loyal to those he loved. And that left Sebastian.

Sebastian was the smoking gun in this scenario.

Wayne sighed, his throat burning as he gulped more whisky. Sebastian's vehicle peeled away from the house. He hoped like hell Sebastian didn't drive off the road on the way to wherever he was going. Sighing again, he topped up his glass and went in search of Jen.

The Thirsty Cricket was busy for a Thursday night, which pissed off Sebastian. He pushed his way to the bar, ordered a beer with a bourbon chaser, found an empty seat and settled in to numb his mind. He downed the bourbon and indicated he wanted another. The competent barman filled his order and kept an attentive eye on him for the rest of the evening, refilling his glass when required. Good man.

Luke Morgan, Sloan's head cop, came up to the bar with James Bates, one of the owners of Fancy Free, the condom company. "Hey, Sebastian. Come and sit with us. We have a table out the back."

"I'm not good company."

"Doesn't matter," James said.

Sebastian didn't miss the silent exchange between the two friends.

"It's a woman-free zone," Luke said. "We're shooting pool."

"Come on," James said. "We're losing badly and need someone to help us out."

"Speak for yourself. I'm not a crap pool player," Luke said.

Sebastian found himself relocating, following in the wake of James as he navigated the crowd on the dance floor. He tripped and staggered, only keeping his feet because Luke grabbed him by the scruff of his T-shirt.

"Easy there." Luke didn't release him until Sebastian took a seat. Beer sloshed from his glass when he set it down, but he didn't spill a drop of the bourbon.

"Woman problems?" James asked, taking possession of the opposite seat.

"Man and woman," Sebastian blurted before his brain engaged. "Shit." He shook himself. "Pretend you didn't hear that."

"Hear what?" Luke queried.

Sebastian sank back into the faux leather seat and tried to relax. No amount of even breathing helped to settle the roiling in his gut. He closed his eyes and saw Jen swollen with child. Every muscle in his body tensed. Fuck! He forced his eyes open and stared at his drink instead. "Who are we playing pool against?"

"Him." Luke jerked his thumb in the direction of the tables. "I'd like to knock him on his pretty city-boy arse."

"Can't do that," James said. "You're a cop."

"Not on duty," Luke pointed out.

"Let's do this." Sebastian was all for kicking butt. Anything to help settle the angst seething inside him.

"Can he shoot straight?" James whispered.

"Heard that," Sebastian said. "Right here you know."

"Can you shoot straight?" Luke asked.

"Straight enough to whip your arse."

Luke nodded. "Let's do this."

Not only was the man a pretty city-boy with his salon-styled blond hair, he was a wise-arse too. And his friend wasn't much better. Wayne didn't like City Boy's friend. Sebastian knew that.

He and Luke settled in to play pool. The city boy broke and slotted in a ball, looking out of place in his suit and business shirt even if he had lost the tie. Two balls later, he missed, handing the table over to Sebastian. Although he was drunk, Sebastian potted several balls before a tricky shot proved the better of him. On his next turn, Sebastian dropped the last two balls before lining up the black. Not an easy shot, but he hit it sweetly and it dropped into the hole.

"Yes!" Luke pumped his fist in the air.

"Rematch," the city boy insisted.

"Rack 'em." Luke accepted the challenge. "Hey, sweetheart." Luke hugged his wife Janaya hello.

"Are you winning?"

"Yep," Luke said, winking at Sebastian.

Another woman sauntered up to the pool table, her familiar perfume making Sebastian stiffen. "What do you want?" he growled at Victoria, his ex.

"Nothing you can give me," she retorted, and she wrapped her arms around the city boy, giving him a passionate kiss before pulling back to fire a malicious smile in Sebastian's direction.

Something tightened inside him. He turned away, ignoring her to hand the cue to Luke. "You break."

Luke made a creditable job of it, giving them a good start and leaving a tricky shot for the city boy.

"A kiss for good luck," Victoria cooed.

Sebastian ignored them and worked to keep the old memories at bay. Bitter memories. Hurt and pain. No matter what he did, he couldn't stop the agonizing thoughts of the past pushing at him. He swallowed and wandered back to the table to have some liquid courage.

Janaya cocked her head. "You okay?"

"No," Sebastian said.

"That won't help."

"Can't hurt," Sebastian said.

"Where's Wayne?" James asked.

"Home." His mouth twisted when he realized what he'd said. After tonight he might not have a home with Wayne. And Jen... Damn, he couldn't sit by and let her get rid of a baby.

"Your turn." Luke handed him the cue stick.

Sebastian studied the balls on the table and got to work.

One after another, he slotted them into the pockets until only the black was left. He sank that too. "Looks as if you lose again," he said to the city boy.

"Don't be such an arsehole," Victoria cried.

"Butt out," Sebastian snapped.

"Don't talk to my fiancée like that," City Boy said.

"Fiancée? I hope you know what you're letting yourself in for." Sebastian blasted Victoria with the full force of his derision. "She's a liar and a cheat."

"Shut up!" Victoria screamed. Her fists flailed out and she collected Sebastian on the nose.

"Bitch."

"Did you hear what he called me?" Victoria demanded.

City boy didn't answer, punching Sebastian instead. Pain reverberated through his jaw. Sebastian fingered the sore spot and wriggled his jaw back and forth. He grinned. "Can't you do better than that?"

City Boy threw another punch. It was wild. Sebastian ducked to the side and punched back. He connected. City Boy went down with a crash.

Victoria slapped Sebastian. "Why did you hit him?" Her hand slashed through the air again. Sebastian tripped while backing up to avoid her. The urge to hit her back was strong but he ignored it. Despite the provocation, he'd never hit her during their marriage and he wasn't about to start now.

"Someone call the cops," Victoria screamed. Her hand lashed out and her fingernails ripped a gouge in his chin. Blood dripped to the floor but Victoria didn't let up.

"He mightn't be able to hit you but I can," Janaya said.

"No weapons," Luke mumbled from behind.

Before Sebastian could start to puzzle that one out, Janaya approached Victoria. Her hands snapped out. Victoria broke off mid-screech when Janaya's fists met their target. Seconds later it was over. Victoria was out cold on the floor and silence reigned.

"I've still got it," Janaya said to Luke.

"Got what, sweetheart? I didn't see a thing."

"Thanks," Sebastian said.

"No problem." Janaya dusted off her hands on the back of her jeans. "Why did you divorce her anyway?"

"She aborted my baby without discussing it with me," Sebastian said, the pain as deep now as it had been when it happened two years ago. Tears pricked at his eyes and he had to blink rapidly to keep control. "And later I discovered she'd cheated." What the fuck? Why was he telling her? He hadn't even told Wayne about the baby.

"I'm sorry." Janaya scowled down at Victoria. "I would have punched her harder if I'd known."

A startled laugh burst from Sebastian. He was glad

Janaya wasn't gunning for him.

"Where's Sebastian?" Jen asked as she slid onto one of the barstools at the kitchen counter.

"I don't know. He didn't come home last night."

"Should we be worried?"

"He's not answering his phone."

Jen frowned. "Any idea where he might be?"

"I'm hoping he turns up here soon, but if he doesn't I'll start at the pub. How are you?"

Jen felt her face crumple, an accompanying tremor slipping through her. "Pregnant."

"I thought you were on the Pill."

"I am," she snapped. "Evidently I hit the percentage that it doesn't work for. Lucky me."

"Whoa." Wayne lifted his hands in a gesture of surrender. "I'm sorry."

"Why don't you ask your next question? Who's the daddy?"

"Jen." Wayne rounded the counter and lifted her off the barstool before wrapping her in the comfort of his arms. "I know you'd never sleep with anyone other than me or Sebastian. What do you want to do?"

"I don't know." Once again emotions overwhelmed her and exited as big, fat tears. They slipped down her cheeks and soaked into Wayne's T-shirt. "My mother would be so angry with me. I feel as if I've let her down. Broken my promise to her."

"I doubt you'd ever disappoint her. My grandmother always says that life doesn't go according to plan. What we need to do is make a new plan. One that you can live with."

Jen sniffed. "You make it sound so easy."

"I know it won't be easy. There are three of us and people are going to speculate."

"I hate gossip. When I was a kid I used to hear people whispering about my mother and how she had an affair with a married man."

"Do you know who your father is?"

"No, whenever I asked my mother brushed it aside. I have no idea. She'd been at university before her pregnancy, so it could have been anyone."

"That's one thing we all have in common then. Sebastian doesn't know anything about his real parents. I have a mother listed on my birth certificate but no father."

"How come Sebastian doesn't know anything?"

"He was abandoned. A couple walking their dog heard him crying. Someone had dumped him in one of those big rubbish bins."

"Oh god. Wayne. That's terrible."

"Yeah. He doesn't talk about it much, but I'm sure that's part of the reason he ended up married to Victoria. He wanted a family."

Some of Sebastian's vehemence of the prior evening started to make sense. "I would never desert a child."

"I know you wouldn't. What *do* you want to do?"

"I'd better go to see a doctor, and I'll go from there."

Wayne smiled down at her and wiped the moisture off one cheek. "That's a good start. Do you want me to come with you?"

"No, you should find Sebastian. I might ring Gaby and ask her to go with me."

"Good plan. Do you want something to eat?"

"No," she said sharply, her stomach going into somersaults at the mention of food. "Maybe a couple of cream crackers."

Wayne grabbed his keys, attempting to hide his worry. "If you're set, I might try to track down Sebastian."

Jen sent him a sharp look. "You're worried."

"Damn, I'm gonna have to work on hiding my emotions a bit better."

"No. It's just that I know you so well."

Ten minutes later, Wayne dropped Jen off at Gaby's.

Neither Gaby, Fletch or Liam had seen Sebastian. He drove to the pub and pulled up beside Sebastian's vehicle. Wayne climbed out of his car, half expecting to see Sebastian sleeping inside his truck. He wasn't. The vehicle was locked.

Damn. Where next? He tried Sebastian's cell phone again, and it went straight to voicemail. He climbed back into his car and drove around town trying to think where Sebastian could be. Nothing. He drove to their office and searched there. Again, nothing.

After exhausting every possibility, he pulled up outside the police station, his gut churning with trepidation.

Luke Morgan, one of the Sloan cops was arriving just as he entered the police station.

"Hey, Luke. I don't suppose you've seen Sebastian?"

"I have. He was in my spare bedroom, snoring fit to wake the dead when I left the house."

"He stayed at your place last night?"

"Yeah. He'd had a skin full, and I decided it might be best." Luke grinned suddenly. "There was a bit of trouble."

"Is he okay?"

Luke's grin widened. "He'll have a headache."

Luke wasn't telling him everything. "Should I go and collect him?"

"Are you the man part of his woman and man trouble?"

Wayne hesitated. "Yes," he said finally.

"Are you gonna sort it out?"

Was he? Wayne considered that for a few seconds then nodded. "Yes."

"Then go and get him," Luke said.

"Thanks." Wayne headed off feeling more confused than ever. At Luke's place, he knocked on the door.

Janaya answered and smiled, her violet eyes twinkling. "You've come to pick up Sebastian."

"Yes. Where is he?"

"Still sound asleep. Down there." She gestured. "Second door on the left."

Wayne slipped off his boots and entered the house. At the doorway of the bedroom Janaya had indicated, he came to a halt. A slow smile curved his lips. Sebastian lay stretched out, wearing just his boxer-briefs, his right arm wrapped around a black and white spotted dog. Wayne chuckled. The pair looked cute and he whipped out his cell phone intending to snap a photo. Before he could take the shot, the dog's eyes popped open. A series of short barks, followed by a hair-raising growl, issued from her throat.

Janaya came running. "Ah, I wouldn't take that photo if I were you. Killer doesn't like having her photo taken."

The dog barked again. A series of sharp barks as if it were

agreeing with Janaya.

Wayne put his phone away and the dog visibly relaxed.

"Come on, Killer. We'll make another pot of coffee."

"Wayne?"

"You're awake," Wayne said.

The dog growled as it wriggled.

"I think she wants you to lift your arm," Janaya said.

Wayne took a quick two steps to the bed and grabbed Sebastian. He hugged him, relief filling him because Seb was safe. In that moment he knew that he had to do everything he could to make them into a family. And most of all, he had to help make Seb feel secure.

Uncaring of the audience, he kissed Sebastian smack on the lips. The man smelled like a pub and didn't taste the best, but Wayne didn't care. This was right where he wanted to be, and every relationship he'd had to date paled in comparison.

He heard the dog give another series of barks and lifted his head.

"Shush, Killer. It's not wrong for men to kiss if they care for each other."

Wayne smiled against Seb's neck. He cared for Sebastian.

The dog barked.

"No, if Luke tried kissing James, I'd brain him. Come, Killer."

The dog scurried after Janaya, leaving them in peace.

Weird. Wayne shrugged away Janaya's strange discussion with the dog. "I was worried about you." He pulled back to study Sebastian properly. "What happened to your face? You have a bruise and is that a scratch?"

"I got in a fight last night in the pub. Victoria hit me."

"And you didn't hit back."

"I can't hit a woman, Wayne." Sebastian sounded shocked.

"Of course you can't, but that doesn't mean she can thump you either."

Sebastian let out a husky chuckle. "No, but Janaya slugged her. You should have seen her. One punch and Victoria went down."

"Was Luke there?"

"He didn't see a thing."

"Coffee is ready," Janaya said from behind them. "What Sebastian means is that Luke pretended he didn't see anything."

"Good for him."

When they walked into the kitchen the dog was barking again. Wayne shook his head. Strange creature. It never seemed to shut up.

"I think they have a girlfriend too," Janaya said.

"Are you talking with that dog?" Wayne asked.

Janaya winked. "Of course I am. Dogs can talk."

Sebastian snorted and dropped onto the nearest chair. "Man, my head hurts."

"Take a couple of these." Janaya handed him two tablets and a glass of water. "My aunt swears by them."

"So you're both with Jen Alexander. She's a nice girl."

"Yeah, she is," Wayne said.

"Where is Jen?"

"She's gone to see the doctor."

Sebastian lurched to his feet. "She hasn't gone to get an abortion?"

"What? Of course not. Seb, sit back down. You should know better. Jen would never have an abortion."

"What is she going to the doctor for then?"

Janaya handed them both mugs of black coffee and shunted milk and sugar in their direction so they could fix their coffees as they pleased. "She's probably gone to confirm the pregnancy and to make sure she's healthy. Right?"

"Yes. Jen might be upset about a baby right now but she won't do anything silly."

"Sebastian, you should tell Wayne," Janaya said.

"Tell me what?"

"Victoria got pregnant and had an abortion without telling me," Sebastian said.

"Fuck! Seb, why didn't you tell me?" That explained his attitude toward the pregnancy.

"I couldn't." Sebastian scowled. "It still kills me every time I think about it."

"Jen isn't Victoria," Wayne said.

The dog barked, and Janaya shushed her. When the dog barked again, Janaya went to the fridge and pulled out a huge bone. After unwrapping it, she gave the treat to the dog. Killer exited via the door.

"What does Jen want to do?" Sebastian asked. "If she doesn't want the baby then maybe she'd consider letting me adopt it."

Sympathy and love clutched at Wayne's chest, making it difficult to draw breath. A thought occurred and he tossed it around in his mind. Yeah, that might work. He'd think on it. "Let's go home. We'll talk with Jen and help her make plans."

"Thanks for looking after me last night, Janaya."

"No problem." She waved off Sebastian's thanks with a flap of her hand. "That's what friends are for."

"Thank you," Wayne mouthed and he set down his coffee to guide Sebastian outside. It was time to go home.

Chapter Thirteen

Sebastian's head thumped like a bitch. He patted his pocket by habit, searching for his sunglasses.

"Here." Wayne handed him his sunnies without Sebastian saying a word.

"Thanks, man."

Jen and Gaby were in the kitchen when they arrived home.

"I thought you were going to the doctor," Sebastian said.

"They were booked solid this morning. I have an appointment for this afternoon."

"Can I go with you?" Sebastian asked.

Jen stared at him for an instant, shot a quick glance at Wayne then nodded. "You can drive me."

Sebastian's breath eased out. "I'll wait for you in the waiting room." Some of the fear encasing him lifted at her agreement. With those few words, she'd let him in, and it meant the world to him.

WAYNE'S FATHER'S BIRTHDAY PARTY

"Wayne, you're here," his mother said. "And this must be Jen." She grasped both of Jen's hands and scrutinized her from head to foot. "You must be doing something right, my son. Your girl is glowing."

Beside him, Sebastian stiffened, and Wayne cursed under his breath. A few careless words and all the frank, honest discussions they'd had during the past week seemed far away. The rest of the world intruded big-time.

"Sebastian," his mother said, inclining her head.

This time it was Wayne who froze. It was about time his mother started treating Sebastian better. Honestly, sometimes she carried on like a queen graciously giving a poor man an audience. Wayne needed to set her straight, although it was something he wasn't looking forward to.

"Where's Dad?" Wayne carried a present the three of them had picked out a few days earlier.

"He's holding court out the back. Put the present in the front room. He's going to open them later this afternoon. Come with me. I want to introduce Jen to the rest of the family."

"I'll take it," Sebastian said, his tone lacking any sort of emotion.

When Sebastian went to take the present off him, Wayne swung his arm around Sebastian's shoulder in a swift, reassuring hug. Their gazes clashed and Sebastian gave a faint nod.

"What are you doing hugging Sebastian?" one of his aunts asked, walking up behind them. "Anyone would think that you're gay."

Sebastian froze. He glared at Wayne's aunt but to Wayne's relief didn't say anything. The last thing they needed today was a shouting match.

"There's nothing wrong with gay," Jen said.

Oh hell. Wayne waited for the fallout.

"It's not right," his aunt said, scowling. "It's against God's laws."

Jen pressed her lips together.

"I'll see you later," Sebastian said and made his escape.

Wayne wished he could do the same. With his hand in the curve of Jen's back, he ushered her after his mother. Gay discussion diverted. For now at least.

"Gerrard." Jen came to an abrupt halt.

Immediately the tension ramped up inside Wayne again. He'd tried to contact Gerrard for the last week, but he'd been away in Taupo with Stan and Justin. Heck, his mother had said Gerrard wasn't going to be here today, and she hadn't been happy about it. Obviously, she'd managed to change Gerrard's mind. Either that or guilt him to death. Wayne was betting on the latter.

"Wayne." Gerrard glowered at Jen. "I need to talk to you."

"Later," Wayne said. "Mum wants to introduce Jen around."

"It's important," Gerrard said, following them outside. He came to an abrupt halt and almost caused a human pileup behind him. "What's he doing here?"

"Aw, hell," Wayne muttered.

Jen squeezed his arm. "Sebastian said—"

"I know what Sebastian friggin' said," Wayne snapped. "Fuck," he breathed. "Sorry. Go and stand with Sebastian. I'll head off Gerrard before he does anything stupid."

"Sebastian and Jen are having an affair behind your back," Gerrard declared in a loud voice.

Everyone fell silent.

"Too late," Jen said.

"You! You cheated on my son with him?" Wayne's mother demanded.

"Mum, listen to me," Wayne said urgently. "Gerrard doesn't understand."

"Sebastian, leave my house. Out! Right now and don't

come back."

"Don't be such a drama queen, Mum. I told you. It's not like that."

Sebastian stiffened, anguish chasing across his face before he blanked his expression. "I'm sorry. This was a bad idea."

"I'd better go too," Jen said.

"That's an excellent idea." Gerrard fired dislike at Jen and Seb.

"No, stay," Wayne said. "Please."

"But Sebastian— No, I'll talk to you later." Strain glittered in her eyes, and he watched her hand rise and smooth across her stomach.

Wayne finally nodded. Jen would be uncomfortable for the rest of the afternoon. Besides, Jen was right. Sebastian needed her more than he did. Despite the audience, he gave her a swift hug and whispered in her ear. "I'm sorry. Tell Sebastian I'm sorry, and I'll be home as soon as I can." He plucked his keys out of his pocket and handed them to her.

"How will you get home?"

"Don't worry about me. Take care." Wayne gave her an encouraging smile and watched her until she disappeared from sight.

"What is going on, Wayne?" his mother asked.

Wayne sighed. "Nothing, Mum." Nothing he could talk

about right now with all the friends and relations around. They'd already heard enough to feed gossip for the next month. "I'll go and say hello to Dad."

The hours passed, and all Wayne could think about was Sebastian and Jen. He'd been stupid to expect Gerrard to keep quiet. Idiotic to expect everything to go smoothly at a family gathering. Yeah, fuckin' dense to believe he could keep his relationship with Jen and Sebastian secret. It wasn't that he was ashamed. No, the truth was he'd guessed the probable reactions of family and friends. He was happy and he hadn't wanted to mess with that. Too late.

Late in the afternoon he managed to corner Gerrard. "You couldn't have talked to me in private?"

"I thought you should know," Gerrard said in a sullen tone. "You shouldn't shoot the messenger."

"The messenger didn't have the facts," Wayne snapped.

"I saw Sebastian kissing Jen, and she was kissing him back."

"You should have knocked."

Gerrard glared back. "I forgot. I never had to knock before."

There was no way around this. "Jen, Sebastian and I are together."

"Yeah. So?"

Wayne stared at Gerrard, waiting for his brother's brain to fire. "Together in a sexual way."

"You?" Gerrard's mouth dropped open. "You and Sebastian share Jen?"

Wayne gave a clipped nod, hesitating before deciding to spit it out. "And each other."

Gerrard glanced both ways then leaned closer. "You're gay?"

"No!" And he wasn't. He loved Sebastian, but other men didn't do a thing for him. "Just Sebastian and Jen."

"Mum's gonna have a cow."

"She'll have to deal with it."

Gerrard shifted his weight from side to side. "Aw, man. I'm sorry for blurting it out like that. I should have spoken to you in private."

"You need to apologize to Sebastian and Jen."

"I'll do it when I drive you home," Gerrard promised.

"Wayne. Gerrard. Come and say goodbye to your uncle and aunt," his mother called.

Gradually the relatives left. His mother and sisters bustled around cleaning and restoring things to their proper place.

"Are you all right, son?"

Wayne started, the hand on his shoulder taking him by surprise. He turned to face his father, a tall, powerful man who still ran several times a week. "I was miles away."

"I heard what happened. Do you love the girl?"

"Yes." There was no doubt in his mind. He loved Sebastian too, and because of that he intended to tell his parents the truth before he left today. He owed it to Sebastian and Jen. He owed it to himself.

"Dad, why does Mum hate Sebastian so much?"

His father frowned, his forehead creasing into a multitude of lines. "She doesn't hate him."

"Could've fooled me."

His father scanned their surroundings. "I saw you hug him."

"Dad, we're a threesome. Sebastian and Jen weren't doing anything wrong when Gerrard saw them."

The air whistled between his father's pursed lips. "We'd better sit down, son."

Wayne followed his father over to a bench seat at the far end of the garden. "You look good, Dad." And his father did. He wore his sixty-five years well, his hair still mostly black with a sprinkle of gray at the temples.

"Before I met your mother, she dated a white man for a few months. One day she smiled at his friend. It was innocent, but the man took exception and thought your mother was cheating. He hit her." His father took a harsh breath as if seeking calm, and instinctively, Wayne reached

225

for his father's hand to offer silent comfort. "And then he raped her."

Wayne gasped, feeling as if someone had struck him in the chest.

"That's why she couldn't have children. Your mother is a strong woman. That man, he broke her, but your mother went to counseling, and we've had a good marriage."

"But I don't understand what this has to do with Sebastian."

"She told me the man who raped her had pale eyes like Sebastian's. She looks at Sebastian and she remembers things she's worked hard to forget."

His father fell silent, and Wayne swallowed, attempting to hold himself together. He'd never suspected his mother's past held such violence and pain.

"She told me I shouldn't play with Sebastian." Although he hadn't been old, the memory of that day had stayed with him over the years.

"I know, son. She told me and she was deeply ashamed of herself for saying it."

"I can't give up Sebastian."

"You were pretty stubborn about it as a child. I wouldn't expect anything less now."

"What should I do?"

"Don't do anything, son. Kiss her goodbye as if nothing

has happened. I'll talk to her."

"She won't approve," Wayne said. It was part of the reason he'd wanted to keep things private.

His father sighed. "Truthfully, I'm not sure I approve, but life is too short to fight. I will reserve judgment."

Wayne understood. He truly did, but now that he was an adult he intended to live his life as he saw fit. While he might have started off without a full plan, he had one now.

"Jen is pregnant, Dad."

"Oh." His father's brown eyes twinkled. "That might help."

"And if the baby is white with blue eyes?"

"Will that matter to you?"

"No." Wayne didn't hesitate in his answer.

"A grandchild won't hurt. Your mother loves children."

Wayne nodded, knowing this truth. His parents had adopted six children in total and fostered others over the years. His mother had a big heart, and he had to pray that she would come around in time.

"WAYNE'S BACK," SEBASTIAN SAID.

Thank goodness. Jen needed Wayne's backup to deal with Sebastian. He hadn't smiled once since they'd returned to the house.

"Gerrard is with him."

"Crap," Jen said with feeling. "I don't want to deal with his dramatics."

"It might be all right. They're laughing at something."

Jen stood and turned to face the door, tension swirling within her. She had enough to worry about without Wayne's family throwing in their opinions. Every time she closed her eyes she pictured her mother and the promises she'd made to her, and she didn't see how she could keep them now that she was pregnant. And then there was her love for Sebastian and Wayne. She couldn't refute it—her love simply was, and she couldn't turn it off even if she tried.

Gerrard came forward immediately. "Jen, I'm sorry about the way I've behaved and what I said today. Please forgive me."

"I wish you'd talked to Wayne first," Jen said, not willing to let him off too easily.

Gerrard smiled, flashing his dimples. "I'm young and stupid. I have to learn these things as I go."

"Yeah, well. You shouldn't upset a pregnant woman," Jen muttered.

"Pregnant?"

"Yes, and I intend to cry all over you every time I get

emotional," Jen vowed, brightening. "Payback."

"But everyone will think that I'm the father." Gerrard sounded appalled at the prospect.

"Too bad," Jen said with a wicked grin. "Payback."

"Shit," Gerrard muttered. "See you next term. Can I tell Stan and Justin about the baby?"

"Just the baby," Wayne said. "Nothing else okay?"

"They'll ask questions," Gerrard warned.

"Tell them you don't know," Wayne ordered. "Thanks for the ride home."

Gerrard cast a cheeky grin at his brother then shared it with her and Sebastian too. "I know when I'm not wanted. See ya." He waved and left.

"Was it rough?" Sebastian asked.

"No worse than it was for you guys. I could do with a drink." Wayne grabbed two beers from the fridge. "Jen, what would you like?"

"Tea, please."

"I'll make it," Sebastian volunteered.

"So what happened?" Jen asked.

"Dad told me some private stuff," Wayne said, and started talking.

By the time he'd finished, Jen felt grudging sympathy for his mother.

"Maybe I should get contact lenses." Despite Sebastian's

joking tone, Jen could see the grim acceptance beneath his exterior. He thought this was the end for them.

"Don't be silly," Wayne said. "She'll get used to the idea eventually. Besides, we've been friends for years, and I'm not about to let my mother's experiences color my relationship with both of you. I've been thinking about this all afternoon and I've come up with a plan."

Sebastian swallowed audibly, and Jen's heart broke for him. Unable to help herself, she stood and went to him. "Let me sit on your knee."

"To help stem gossip about Jen's pregnancy, I think you and Jen should get married."

Sebastian frowned. "But what about you?"

"Nothing needs to change between us. I love both of you guys. A marriage will help people accept the baby. But we can have a second, private ceremony with our friends where the three of us can confirm our love for each other. Do rings and everything. A honeymoon during Jen's next term break."

"I'll be as big as a house by then," Jen objected.

"You love us," Sebastian declared, sounding much happier.

"I do. I've changed," Wayne said with a grin. "I don't fuck just anyone these days."

"You haven't fucked me," Sebastian said bluntly.

"But we're getting there," Wayne said seriously. "And I want to. When the three of us are together it's special. And when I'm with either you or Jen alone it's still special. That's what I'm saying. I love both of you, and I'm not backing off. No matter what our friends and neighbors say or my family, I'm in this relationship for the long haul."

"But marriage?" Sebastian asked.

Wayne glanced at her, and Jen got it. Of the three of them Sebastian needed security most. A legal marriage would help give him that security.

"I love you both, and I'm afraid you're stuck with me. Besides, one of you has to make an honest woman of me."

A frown creased Sebastian's brow. "But Jen, what about your studies? Do you want to keep the baby?"

"Yes." During her initial panic she'd considered abortion, but she couldn't do it, and now Sebastian's approval made her glad.

"I've been thinking about this too," Wayne said. "Between the three of us we can afford childcare. Jen can still go to varsity. We can get an apartment up in town or we can work out some way for you to commute. Gerrard told me he's going to varsity next year. If your schedules mesh, he won't mind taking you with him."

"And we'll do a proper ceremony for the three of us?" Sebastian asked, his large hand covering her stomach in a protective manner. She didn't even think he was aware of it, but his touch warmed her through.

"Yes," Jen said, Wayne's sincerity winning her over. "We'll make it extra special so we'll never forget that the three of us are a unit." It might not be easy, but if they all pulled together, it might work. "I could look into part-time study too. As long as I'm working toward my degree I'll feel as if I'm honoring my promise to my mother."

"Stand," Sebastian said, gently shifting her off his lap. "Wayne, come over here."

"What for?"

"Just do it," Sebastian ordered. When both she and Wayne stood in front of Sebastian, the harshness left his face, replaced by a tender smile that lit his pale eyes. "Jen. Wayne. I love you both. Will you marry me?"

Chapter Fourteen

Three weeks later

"Do you, Jennifer Isabel Alexander, take Wayne Jefferson Garrett and Sebastian Lang as your husbands?"

Jen gave both men a broad smile. "I do."

The celebrant continued, apparently unfazed by marrying three people. Jen glanced at Wayne and Sebastian and her heart swelled with love. This ceremony meant everything to her, even though it wasn't a legal one. It meant way more than the non-personal one that had married her and Sebastian in law.

"I now pronounce you men and wife," the celebrant said, hesitating at this final part. "You may now kiss the bride?"

Wayne and Sebastian didn't dawdle. They crowded her, surrounding her front and back before kissing each other.

In the background Jen heard laughter and cheering, but she was too busy enjoying the moment. The combination changed and she scored kisses from both her men.

Once the kissing ended, they turned to face their friends. Both men held her hands, and Jen couldn't have said which man bore the widest grin.

"Now we party," Sebastian said.

It was the cue for everyone to converge on them to offer congratulations. It was the happiest day of Jen's life.

THANK YOU FOR READING *Buzz*. Did you enjoy it? If so, please consider leaving a review at your favorite online bookstore. A review would make my day!

Turn the page for an excerpt from *Safeguarding Sorrel*, the next story in the *Fancy Free* series. The eagle-eyed amongst you might have noticed that officially *Safeguarding Sorrel* is part of the *Military Men* series. That's true, but this steamy romance is a standalone and it is set in the *Fancy Free* world.

Excerpt – Safeguarding Sorrel

Sloan, a country town in New Zealand

Sorrel Thyme peered through the scratchy bushes, desperately trying to ignore the sand flies making a meal of her bare arms. This had to be one of the world's most uncomfortable ways to score a job interview.

The man and woman she was spying on started to kiss—a passionate no-holds-barred kind of kiss. Horrified, she watched hands steal beneath clothes, gulped as busy fingers squeezed and caressed.

The amount of flesh on display increased, and she squirmed, heat whooshing through her body to explode in her face. Talk about embarrassing. She wasn't sure what to do, where to look. Alice and James Bates, the owners of the Fancy Free condom company, didn't have a mere picnic on their minds. Oh, no. They were busy tearing off each other's clothes, right in front of her.

Aghast, she squeezed her eyes shut, her skin crawling from exposure to the bugs. It was the only way to explain the edgy sensation blooming inside her, prickling across her skin, irritating her breasts.

The sharp evergreen scent of the totara and manuka trees wafted to her, refreshing and aromatic. Her stomach let out a feisty rumble of complaint, and she jerked in panic. The bushes concealing her rustled, and her eyes flew open. She froze, horror filling her at the risk of discovery.

Alice and James continued their amorous activities. Sorrel's breath eased out. She caught a flash of pale breast. At least they were too far away to hear her stomach clamoring for food. Placated by the thought, she eased her weight into a more comfortable position. The bush played a musical tune against her robe, and a branch cracked beneath her right foot.

"What was that?" Alice's voice carried across the clearing.

Sorrel bit back a moan of dismay, her gaze darting this way and that to determine the damage. If she didn't move, didn't answer perhaps they'd decide a restless bird loitered in the trees. *I promise to leave the instant they settle again. Please let them continue.* Maybe she'd manage to retreat with her dignity intact.

This was a bad idea. A stupid one. How she'd ever thought—

"Who's there?" James was on his feet now, putting his jeans to rights and staring in her direction. "I know there's someone there. You might as well come out."

Intent on self-preservation, Sorrel sprang to her feet, adrenaline kicking in big-time. She cried out as cramp struck in a painful surge, staggered two steps. Her robe snagged tight on a bush. Held fast, she panicked, yanking fabric free, frantic to escape.

Then he was on her, tackling her from behind. She hit the ground. A pained grunt escaped, the air exploding from her lungs. A hand closed around her leg, and seconds later, his weight held her in place.

"Let me go." She flailed. Ineffectually, as it happened. James Bates was one big dude.

"Who is it?" Alice called.

"A woman."

He shifted his weight, and Sorrel could breathe again. She sucked in a huge draft of air and gathered herself, ready to flee.

"Not so fast." James grasped her upper arm and yanked her around to face him. His bright blue eyes held an edge of anger that had her quaking in her sandals. He dragged her into the clearing where Alice stood with her arms crossed protectively over her chest.

Sorrel couldn't meet their gazes. She straightened her robe, brushing off the dry leaves and dirt. Her hands trembled while panicked thoughts buzzed through her mind like a swarm of bees in a tizzy about honey theft.

Job interview.

Not going well.

This was a bad, bad idea.

With escape looming large in her mind, she slid a furtive glance to her left.

"You're from the Children of Nature cult."

Give the man a prize. Sorrel twisted her hands together, her grubby robe brushing her bare legs. She had others the same, albeit cleaner, hanging on the rack in the shared wardrobe at the single women's quarters. The white robe was a dead giveaway of her status.

Cult member.

Woman.

Trapped.

"Yes." She aimed for a crisp tone. Instead her reply emerged young and scared. Terrified, which was nothing but the truth because the noose was already around her neck. Day by day it tightened, threatening to choke the life from her.

"Why are you spying on us?" Alice's brown hair stood in tousled peaks, her face pale beneath its sprinkling of golden freckles. "Is this a new angle—another campaign to smear Fancy Free?"

Sorrel swallowed, still prepared to flee the second James loosened his grip. But her legs trembled, her knees threatening to crumple like flimsy paper, not up to the job of holding her weight. She'd give anything to turn back the clock ten minutes. *No.* She had their attention—the opportunity she'd schemed and plotted for. It was time to embrace courage.

She sucked in a fortifying hit of tree-laced air, striving for calm. "I wasn't spying. I have no intention of hurting your company or...or haranguing you about the evils of condoms and birth control." *Better.* Her voice quavered only a fraction this time.

"You were spying through the bushes," James snapped. "Do you have a camera?"

A startled laugh burst from her. "Where would I get a camera? I have no money. I didn't mean to spy. Really, I just wanted to talk to you."

"Most people use the phone," James said.

"You don't know much about Children of Nature, do you?" Sorrel owned the clothes on her back—her sole possessions—and even then she wasn't sure she always received the same white robes back from the communal laundry.

"What did you want to discuss?" Alice's tone carried a generous helping of suspicion.

"I've invented a cream. It's similar to a...an aphrodisiac. It enhances sexual pleasure. I want to sell it to your company, in the hope I can raise enough money to strike out on my own and leave Children of Nature." Once she'd started, the words poured from her, one almost running into another in her haste to get them out. "But you can't tell anyone I've offered it to you. You can't tell or they'll steal it from me. You have to promise. You have to promise me you won't tell."

"Shush," Alice said, visibly calmer now. "Have you eaten?"

"I..." Sorrel's stomach let out an embarrassing rumble, forcing the truth from her. "No."

"James, release the girl." Alice offered a kind smile, which settled some of Sorrel's unease. "Come and have something to eat. You can describe your product while we have our lunch."

"I thought we were going to have a private picnic." James

scowled, his brows drawing together in displeasure. His longish dark hair gave him a disreputable air as did the stubble on his face.

Alice reached out and ran her fingertips over his cheek. "I'll make it up to you tonight."

"Promise?"

The clear intimacy between the couple brought discomfort, and Sorrel shuffled from foot to foot, debating whether she should grasp this opportunity or try to make an appointment for a later date.

"With a cherry on top." Alice winked at her husband. "Come." She grasped Sorrel's hand and tugged her to their tartan picnic blanket. "Do you work in the Children of Nature store?"

"No." Sorrel's mouth compressed into a tight line. She used to take her turn working in the store and had enjoyed interacting with the town's people. But that had been before Brother Rick had taken over the running of Children of Nature from his father. That had—

She broke off her thoughts. "No, I make the soap and other products to sell in the store."

"The cult won't let you leave?" James asked, his eyes narrowed on her as if she were untrustworthy and out to take advantage of his wife. She'd seen the way he looked at Alice, as if she was the most important thing in his world.

As a teenager she'd wished someone would gaze at her in that—

Again she put a brake on her thoughts. Thinking of what-if wouldn't help her situation. She had to make her own luck.

"It's difficult to leave if you lack money or contacts in the outside world."

"Sit," Alice said. "Here, you can have my glass. I'll share with James."

Gingerly, Sorrel kneeled and settled herself on the edge of the blanket. Now that she had their ear, fear writhed through her—a ravenous beast. She'd tested her product on herself, but what if her tingly cream didn't work on other women?

"I need to do more tests," she blurted.

"Of course you do." Alice handed her a glass of homemade lemonade and a chicken sandwich. "Eat first, and then we'll talk."

"Who stops you from leaving the cult?"

Alice laughed lightly. "James, do let the girl eat before you decide to grill her."

"They're not trustworthy." James scowled at her. "None of them."

Sorrel's shoulders slumped. "It's all right. I understand your doubts. I'll find another way." Despite her hunger and her disappointment, she placed the sandwich back on the plate and set down the glass of lemonade. "Thank you for listening to me. I'm sorry I interrupted your private time together." She stood and turned away, defeat a heavy sack on her shoulders.

She could hardly blame them. Children of Nature held regular protests outside Alice and James's company, Fancy Free. They organized petitions and talked to everyone who would listen about the evils of condoms—the very product Fancy Free manufactured.

"Wait. You want out." James glanced at his wife in clear speculation. "How far are you willing to go to leave the cult?"

Gasping, Sorrel drew herself up tall, or as tall as a five-foot-three-inch woman could and scowled at him. "I don't do group sex."

Turning away once again, tears of failure smarted at her eyes, but she held her shoulders square and departed. She'd have to find another way, and soon before Brother Rick implemented his plans to partner every woman above twenty-five with a man. There was no doubt in her mind he'd make good on his threats, and her twenty-fifth birthday was a mere two months away. Stars! She couldn't pretend enthusiasm for sex when pregnancy would trap her in the compound.

"We don't participate in group sex, either," Alice said in a wry tone. "One man is more than enough for me to handle. Wait." She jumped to her feet and ran after Sorrel. "Please stay."

Sorrel hesitated, unsure. She cast a doubtful glance over her shoulder, her steps slowing.

"Please, tell us about your cream. Please." Alice smiled in encouragement and led her back to the blanket. "What's your name? You know ours so you have us at a disadvantage."

"Sorrel Thyme. I know your names because I've been part of the picket line outside Fancy Free a time or two." She lifted her chin in faint challenge when they scowled at her words. "It's a change from making products for the shop."

"Glad our condom business offers you rest and relaxation," James muttered.

Alice elbowed her husband and smiled at Sorrel. "Share our food. Tell us what help you want from us."

What does Sorrel want?
Learn what happens next in Safeguarding Sorrel...
www.shelleymunro.com/books/safeguarding-sorrel/

About Author

USA Today bestselling author Shelley Munro lives in Auckland, the City of Sails, with her husband and a cheeky Jack Russell/mystery breed dog.

Typical New Zealanders, Shelley and her husband left home for their big OE soon after they married (translation of New Zealand speak - big overseas experience). A twelve-month-long adventure lengthened to six years of roaming the world. Enduring memories include being almost sat on by a mountain gorilla in Rwanda, lazing on white sandy beaches in India, whale watching in Alaska, searching for leprechauns in Ireland, and dealing with ghosts in an English pub.

While travel is still a big attraction, these days Shelley

SHELLEY MUNRO

is most likely found in front of her computer following another love - that of writing stories of contemporary and paranormal romance and adventure. Other interests include watching rugby (strictly for research purposes), cycling, playing croquet and the ukelele, and curling up with an enjoyable book.

Visit Shelley at her Website
www.shelleymunro.com

Join Shelley's Newsletter
www.shelleymunro.com/newsletter

Follow Shelley at Bookbub
www.bookbub.com/authors/shelley-munro

Other Books by Shelley

Fancy Free
Protection
Romp
Buzz
Festive

Friendship Chronicles
Secret Lovers
Reunited Lovers
Clandestine Lovers
Part-Time Lovers
Enemy Lovers
Maverick Lovers
Sports Lovers

Military Men
Innocent Next Door
Soldiers with Benefits
Safeguarding Sorrel
Stranded with Ella
Josh's Fake Fiancée
Operation Flower Petal
Protecting the Bride

Bundle
Military Men

Alien Encounter series
Janaya
Hinekiri
Alexandre

Bundle
Alien Encounter

www.ingramcontent.com/pod-product-compliance
Lightning Source LLC
Chambersburg PA
CBHW022106240626
47153CB00007B/2258